To Donna

EL MIRADOR

By Jean Maxwell

Special Edition Author's Cut

*your daughter-in-law
has excellent literary
taste! Enjoy —*

Jean Maxwell

03/08/12

ACKNOWLEDGMENTS

Thank you to my family for humouring me and allowing me the time and space to indulge in the creation of this work. For the interest and encouragement to finish it and for not laughing even once.

With grateful thanks to Dawn, Gracie, Debbie, Silva, Lisa and Rosanna, Chris Baty and NaNoWriMo, the helpful critters who inhabit the online creative spaces, the Toronto Romance Writers Association and MacEwan Writing Works.

PROLOGUE

July, 1972

"Don't do it, mi amigo. Le ruego, I'm begging you. No lo hagas, don't do it."

Tristan's hoarse voice echoed in the hollow concrete underground. He gripped Ari's arm, appealing to reason but his friend wrenched away.

Darkness and heat cloyed the space, the smell of petrol thick around them. Black tar oozed from the uneven ground beneath their feet. The flames would rage out of control if Ari set off the acetylene torch he clutched in his sweating hands.

"Ella no vale la pena, Ari. It's not worth it, *she's* not worth it," Tristan said, his tone desperate. Ariel Torres was his friend, his mentor, the accomplished master showing his young apprentice the ropes of the hospitality business. Tristan couldn't bear to watch him destroy everything he'd worked for in a single moment of passion, rage. Jealousy. And for what? A careless woman who didn't love Ari or the unborn child she carried. Ari didn't even know if the baby was his.

"Damn you, Ari. I didn't bail your ass out of that backstreet cantina for this," Tristan shouted, his memory of the night they met flashing back to him. Was this how it happened when you were about to die, images of the past appearing in your mind at random? "I should have let that gypsy bastard kill you then and saved you the trouble!"

The interior of the tiny tavern in Madrid took shape in the young engineer's head, a picture of Torres amid clacking castanets and drunken revelry, ogling and ass-grabbing the red-haired flamenco dancer.

"You know nothing, estudiante!" Ari said with measured contempt, waving the torch at him. "Nothing about life, or women."

What? Tristan Benjamin Flynn, top engineering graduate from Cardiff University, knew nothing? Tristan's fear meshed with anger as he pushed sweaty locks of his blond, lionish mane of hair from his face.

Ari had taught him nearly everything about life since arriving at the Costa del Sol together after that night in Madrid. How dare he say such a thing? He admired Ari, his education, his thriving hotel and casino enterprise, his fast cars and even faster women. Had Tristan been wasting his time hanging about with the likes of him?

The memory pushed its way in again, the bright-coloured swish of the dancer's skirt as she lured Ari into the crooked alleyways of Madrid to be ambushed by the big Romani.

Tristan swung his heavy backpack and coldcocked the hapless brute from behind, saving Ari from a second black eye and worse.

No, Tristan thought, forcing away the parade of the past. *It can't end this way. Not over this.* They'd been friends too long, despite an age difference and Ari's perpetual recklessness, to give up on their dreams now.

They'd lived the high life here, on the famous strip of white beaches, holiday resorts and wild nightlife of the sunny

Spanish coast. They'd learned from and trusted one another. Just yesterday, Ari had pressed money into his hands to gamble in his casino--because Tristan had a knack for winning.

Never had he wanted to win more than now. He needed to persuade Ari not to set fire to the twenty floors of his own hotel above.

He had to find a way to save this place and Ari, too.

"Tristan, sale de aquí," Ariel said with eerie calm, pulling the striker from his pocket.

Tristan didn't move. "You don't mean that, Ari. Come with me, walk away and leave this place."

Ari repeated in English, raising his voice, his eyes glazed with madness. "Get out of here, now! Ahora!" He raised the torch higher and began to open the valve. The escaping fuel made an evil hiss.

Tristan's lungs burned from inhaling the hot air and fumes. He backed away, staring at his friend in horror and defeat.

Then he turned and ran.

CHAPTER ONE

October, 2010

Zara Marlena Flynn leaned forward in the back seat of the moving Mercedes, craning her neck to see better. Awakening from a fitful nap, she blinked away the sleep from her eyes and watched the monstrosity rise from the horizon like a charred skeleton reaching into the air. Black against the azure sky beyond it and the brilliant white beach upon which it stood, she half-wished it might be a mirage that would disappear in a shimmering wave of heat. Instead it drew nearer, enlarging itself unbidden in the car's window.

"This is my inheritance?" she asked. "It's not a hotel. It's hardly even a building." She stared in disbelief at the wall-less slabs of concrete suspended one above the other by vertical columns. Bent, uneven fingers of steel pointed aimlessly upward from its roof. "Someone's made a mistake."

"Es okay, Mees," said Jorge in his strong Spanish accent. He nodded toward the structure as he steered the Mercedes around the wide sweep of motorway that followed the shoreline. "No mistake. This is El Mirador, the property that your father wished you to have."

Zara stared at the forbidding remains of the building. Clearer now, as their approach slowed to within a few hundred meters, she could see the degrading concrete, chipped and blackened with fungi from the moist air off the Mediterranean. She counted, 16, 17...20 stories in all. She supposed there must have been a penthouse at one point, which explained the flailing, loose steel poking out the top.

She sank back into her seat.

"Oh, Jorge, are you sure?" she asked, her voice almost a whine. Jorge was nothing if not honest. He'd worked for Flynn Enterprises, her father's company, for as long as she could remember and now chauffeured her around the Costa del Sol to investigate this legacy left to her.

Such as it was.

"Si, Miss. This is prime resort property. You must look beyond what is apparent," Jorge said, his voice matter-of-fact. "You must have visión, like your father. You are like him. You will see." He swung the car onto an exit ramp off the highway, circling towards the abandoned edifice onto a narrow road where the pavement gave way to crushed gravel and the ubiquitous white sand that surrounded them.

Beautiful, she'd give it that. The beach stretched for miles in both directions, equally breathtaking no matter if you looked left or right, east or west. Lapping waves of the Mediterranean Sea were ever-present. Beckoning, whispering, seducing.

She turned her attention back to the ruined structure. Though stark and sinister-looking now it must have been fabulous in its day, Zara thought. She imagined all sorts of scandalous escapades taking place here while famous celebrities vacationed with abandon. What records she'd been able to find told of the fire that gutted it in the early 70s but she'd presumed it had been rebuilt at least once since then. She swallowed bitterly.

Looks like the joke's on me.

Why her father had acquired it remained a mystery. He'd never spoken of it, at least not to Zara. It seemed she'd been left in the dark until the reading of his will. He'd purchased the property over a year ago but beyond that, there was little information. She knew only that with the sudden loss of its' CEO, Flynn Enterprises needed her.

And she needed answers.

Top engineers like Tristan Flynn didn't just have 'accidents' on the job. And he wouldn't have bequeathed a derelict old building to his daughter without good reason.

Jorge stopped the car. After their long drive, Zara stretched her stiffened legs out the rear door. As she stepped outside, the heat formed an almost physical obstacle barring her way. Her lungs balked at inhaling the superheated air. In a moment, the breeze off the water made its sinuous way toward them and she lifted her long hair off her neck to catch its cooling breath.

Sand slipped inside her sandals. Even her light-coloured linen pantsuit felt uncomfortable in this hot, humid climate.

"We will stay only a moment, Miss. You are not used to the heat and we must get to our hotel soon," Jorge said, taking her arm as they stepped away from the vehicle and towards the dark hulk. There were no safety barricades or caution flags anywhere.

Zara stopped about 50 meters away, gazing at the gaping, non-existent walls, her eyes moving upward to take in the enormity of the thing. Impressive in its own buzzard-like way, it seemed to send echoes of seabird cries and crashing surf drifting over the deserted landscape.

Deserted.

An apt description.

Dad had died thousands of miles away from his family.

She'd not talked to him for months before the accident and felt robbed of that precious time she could have spent with him. The sting of tears returned, as it had so many times when she thought of her father over the past several weeks. Tears of anger as well as sadness. *He knew better than to put himself in danger on a jobsite.*

The irony of it made the news of his death on the Indonesian project very hard to take. She admired her mother for having accepted it with typical Spanish stoicism. Zara used to wonder if Mom had ever regretted leaving her homeland after marrying the dashing and enterprising Tristan B. Flynn. But of course she hadn't--they'd been deeply in love. Still, Dad had been away a lot over the years and though heartbroken, Mom seemed to have known that one day he wouldn't make it home.

Zara stared harder at the remains, raising her hand to her brow to block the glare of the sun. She noted the way the sand drifted up the sides of the base, how the spiny steel points reached heavenward. It reminded her of the half-buried Statue of Liberty in a movie.

A few moments of silence passed with only the sound of the surf as backdrop. "Let's get out of here." *I have a hell of a lot of work ahead.* Turning abruptly, she made her way back to the cool interior of the Mercedes.

*

The car sped eastward, revealing a myriad of views of the Mediterranean coast. Shining beaches one moment, rocky cliffs the next. Villages occasionally dotted the hills to the north, their whitewashed buildings stuck like sugar cubes to the ascending hillside. Slender palm groves lined both sides of the road as they passed hotels and vacation properties.

"Aqui, here we are," Jorge said. He gestured to a white archway looming on the road ahead. As they drew nearer, Zara could see the lettering carved into the archway. MARBELLA. White pillars flanked it, adorned with beautiful plantings of dwarf palms and dracaena, lush pink blooms and draping vines cascading over giant white planter bowls.

Through the partly open window she could smell their intoxicating bouquets mixed with salty sea air as they passed. The clear blue sky made a striking background to the white, etching the name into the viewer's eye.

Once beyond the arch, they entered the town of Marbella. Resorts and residences were visible on either side of the road in continuous succession. White stucco and wrought iron appeared everywhere, as did masses of flowering plants and exotic greenery at every gatepost and doorway.

"This is beautiful," Zara said, shifting towards the window to get a better look. "What is this place?"

"Ah," Jorge answered, "Marbella. The Beverly Hills of Andalusia." He chuckled, waving his upturned hand at the townscape and looking back at her with a wink.

It does look a little Beverly Hills, Zara thought, all that stucco and paving stone, sweeping staircases leading to grand entrances of homes and condominiums set into the rolling landscape. But an old-world graciousness existed here, that no made-in-America movie town could ever match.

The architecture fascinated her. She remembered with dismay the dilapidated wreck she'd just inherited. *Wouldn't it be something to restore it to its former glory?* She pondered the possibility and sheer scope of such a project. Daunting to say the least. She'd know more after the meeting with Flynn's operations manager and local development officials tomorrow.

Zara sighed. She'd given herself until Christmas to make a go of running Flynn Enterprises' operations in this area. She wasn't at all certain about leaving her familiar life in Montreal to take this on. *Have I bitten off too much?* No. She needed to prove herself, challenge herself. She owed Dad this.

The highway began to curve inland, away from the coastline. The land to the south became more mountainous, revealing properties visible along the horizon. Jorge steered the Mercedes into the right-hand lane, preparing to exit off the main road. Soon, Zara could make out a sign, 'Club Marbella, Zona Hotelera.' Jorge took this exit, and ascended the ridge into the hotel zone.

"Are we getting close?" Zara asked. The drive seemed long all of a sudden. It had been several hours since leaving the airport in Seville.

"Si, Miss," Jorge replied. "The gates are just up ahead."

As they reached the top of the road, the Flynn-built Club Marbella revealed itself in all its grandeur. Elegant and exclusive, massive palm trees and elaborate topiaries bordered the surrounding white walls. They pulled up to the huge wrought-iron gates, where gleaming brass letters mounted on either side read 'Club Marbella' in a contemporary script.

The Mediterranean Sea provided a glistening canvas behind. Though not quite sunset, big hurricane lanterns above the lettering glowed with welcoming light, beckoning the Mercedes through the gates.

They cruised up the stone driveway, admiring the beautiful green lawns and charming statuary of angels and animals that peeked out from well-placed shrubbery along its length. They stopped at the glass doors under a covered entrance, where concierges waited to retrieve their luggage. Zara got out of the car and walked into the sumptuous lobby. Ceiling fans revolved overhead in the vaulted interior, making the space humanly comfortable against the heat outdoors.

Despite the palatial environment, Zara wanted only to get to her room and a good night's sleep. While she waited at the desk for her cardkeys, a loud bang echoed from a nearby hallway, followed by the rolling sound of wheels. A set of double doors swung open, and a huge flatbed cart appeared, loaded with audio speakers, instrument cases and other equipment.

One of the two desk clerks ran towards it saying, "Utilice la carga." Thanks to her mother, Zara understood a considerable amount of Spanish and knew this referred to the loading dock. The clerk didn't seem pleased they were bringing in equipment through the main lobby.

"Here you are, Senorita," the female desk clerk said above the noise, handing her the newly coded cards. "Suite 1004. Elevators are izquierda, to your left."

"Gracias," Zara said. Turning to leave, she saw a figure passing quickly on the far side of the equipment cart, a grey hoodie pulled over his head as if trying to escape notice. Two burly companions followed.

The desk clerk gasped. "Dios mío." Zara looked quizzically at her. Wide-eyed, the girl gaped openly at the mysterious passer-by. "Es él, it's him! Es Miguel!" she exclaimed, clapping her hand to her mouth as if she'd said too much.

Chapter Two

Dave Parker paused in the doorway of Ernesto Alvarez' office, a sheaf of fax papers in his hand. A bright and pleasant room, its window overlooked the garden between city hall and the market street. The long centre table lay strewn with blueprints, scale rulers, design notes and drafting setsquares.

Ernesto, Flynn Enterprises' operations manager, stood hunched over a light-table in the corner of the office, flipping overlays on a site plan of some kind. At 8:00am, he'd probably been here an hour already, Dave thought. The man was tireless, always arriving at the office before anyone else. Dave knocked on the open doorframe. Ernesto looked up, pushing his eyeglasses into position.

"Hey Ernie, you wanted to see me," Dave said as he strode into the office. He handed the fax papers to him. "These came for you."

Ernesto smiled. "Gracias, David," he said, moving towards the centre table and reaching to take the papers. "Yes, I have a bit of a job for you."

Dave shoved his hands in his jean pockets and stood facing him. He shrugged at Ernesto's comment and gave him one of his comedic, deadpan expressions. "No kidding, Ern. I do work here, you know."

Ernesto chuckled aloud in response. Dave always seemed able to make him laugh and see the lighter side of things. He knew Ernesto liked him for this reason, among others. But then most people did. Call it a gift. He drew people to him with his disarming sense of humour and easygoing personality.

He'd worked hard to build good relationships with everyone here in the Malaga office of Flynn Enterprises. Had it been three years already? He hoped to move up in the company and had jumped at the chance to work abroad when they'd offered him a transfer from the Boston office. Though still young, as engineers went, Dave felt he'd earned the respect of many senior executives and foremen on the job--including Tristan Flynn himself.

Their interactions had been few but the magnanimous Flynn left a big impression on Dave. Mr. Flynn called him 'Youngblood.' *Hello Youngblood, what do you know today,* he'd say in his charming Welsh accent. *Don't sit down Youngblood, I've moved your chair.*

He missed him. Sometimes painfully so. Dave was the only other person from the Malaga office who'd been to the Indonesian site. *Worse than that.* The only one who'd come back.

Ernesto repositioned his glasses as he prepared to read the printed pages in his hand. "David, I would like you to meet with a new team member and help out with the El Mirador project. Are you busy on Wednesday?"

"I'm always busy, but I have the crews all lined up for this week so whatever you need, I'm sure I can spare some time," Dave said. "What's up at El Mirador?"

Ernesto's expression turned serious and he ran a hand through his steel-gray hair. His eyebrows knitted together as he read the information on the fax sheet. The news didn't seem good.

After a moment Ernesto looked up, peering over the top of his glasses. "The site has a new owner, someone who's also coming to work for Flynn." He paused. "In fact, she *is* Flynn Enterprises now--she's Tristan's daughter," he said, staring pointedly at Dave as if expecting some unusual reaction.

Well, he wouldn't get one if Dave could help it. He drew in a thoughtful breath and folded his arms across his chest. "And?"

"She's also the new CEO of our division and will be heading up the restoration effort. I'm meeting with her in an hour," Ernesto said. "I'd like you to accompany her on a site visit."

"Really," Dave said, allowing a heartbeat of silence to punctuate his words. "So, now I'm a tour guide? I thought you said you wanted help."

Ernesto smiled. "You make it sound boring, David. I'm sure you'll enjoy a break from your desk. And yes, I need your help. She needs your help. Don't let her get too closely involved."

Dave frowned. "If this woman's the new boss, shouldn't she know everything? I mean, full disclosure and all."

Ernesto shrugged one shoulder. "She's travelled a long way and needs time to get settled." He glanced down at the fax he still held. "Just make sure you wear all the proper safety gear and keep an eye on her. She needs to be part of the operation, but from a distance. It's not safe."

"Why?"

"Let me show you." He motioned to the light table. Dave walked around the centre table to join him. "See the foundation plan here, and here," Ernesto said, pointing to adjacent corners of the drawing. "The mechanicals run east to west, steel studs north to south as usual. But here," he circled his finger around the opposite corner of the building on the landward side. "This area is blank, no reinforcement, no pilasters or columns. This is where I think you need to look."

Dave scanned the blueprint. "Look for what?"

Ernesto pulled one of the fax papers from the bundle and handed it to him. "Just let me know what you find. Or, what you don't find."

Dave eyed him narrowly and took the sheet from him. *Oh shit, this again?* They'd talked about it many times, Ernesto's suspicions surrounding the Indonesian job and his fears that the same thing might happen again. He knew what Ernesto wanted him to look for.

"Okay, Ernie. I'll do it," Dave said with resignation. "Don't worry about a thing." Ernesto nodded as he adjusted his eyeglasses again. Dave turned to leave the room. "And make that damn optometrist appointment, man…you drive me nuts with those glasses."

Dave returned to his own office at the opposite end of the hall. Tristan's daughter. Great. A shiny new CEO stepping right off the plane and into the boardroom. She hadn't put in five minutes with the company let alone five years. How would this affect his plans for advancement? And how would he carry out an investigation while ushering her around? Some overfed, spoiled rich kid with Harvard credentials.

At least that's how he pictured her. It occurred to him he hadn't even asked her name.

*

The alarm clock on the nightstand next to Zara's bed began squawking at 7:00 a.m. She slammed the snooze button. Shifting under her covers, not yet aware of her surroundings, she dozed off again until the alarm buzzed once more. Shutting it off completely this time, she reluctantly looked at the LED display.

She felt the crisp linen of the sheets, the silky slipping noise of the satin bedspread as she rolled over onto her side. As she lay, facts seemed to present themselves one by one inside her brain. *Marbella. Spain. Costa del Sol. Meeting this morning.*

Oh yeah.

She heaved the covers aside and made her way to the bathroom. Turning on the shower, she stepped in and watched the water spray against the walls and run in rivulets down the marble tiles. The warm, steamy enclosure made a private, perfect incubator for her thoughts and within its confines, she could give free rein to the memories she'd been keeping at bay.

She missed her father terribly. He'd flown in and out of her life since the day of her birth. The Flynn banner waved on building sites, excavators and cranes all over the world. In spite of its' size, the company had a reputation for 'green' builds, producing high-tech designs with low-impact, earth-friendly methods. Something she could be proud of.

As a child she remembered marvelling at daddy's 'big biddings' and how this fascination led to her degree in architecture from McGill University.

But she'd disappointed him. He'd always expected her to take her place with Flynn Enterprises when she'd graduated, but being Zara, she wanted to make her own way and chose to stay in Montreal and work for a smaller firm. *Great decision,* she thought, mocking herself. A company restructure forced her into unemployment less than a year later.

Shit happens every day. It had nothing to do with her skill or competence. So why did she still feel so…inadequate? She scrubbed her skin with the hotel-issue loofah as if to scrape away the feeling and wash it down the drain with the rest of the suds.

Her mother Marlena had insisted she come home to Barrie after she'd been laid off. She'd had no immediate options at that point anyway. Then came the day…that awful day they got the call.

Zara felt numb as the company lawyer read the will to them. The words 'El Mirador' meant nothing to her then. When it became clear that she would need to make the trip to Spain, Marlena chose to let her daughter take on this new challenge of her inheritance alone.

"When you have taken care of the business," she said, "I will join you. I am longing to see home again." Mom still referred to Spain as home even though she'd lived more than half her life in Canada. A classic beauty, Marlena had done well as both a scholar and a part-time model. This at least, had been Zara's good fortune; blessed with her mother's lovely shape and features.

Too bad this good fortune hadn't extended to her hair.

Unlike Mom's flowing brunette tresses, Zara's sandy-coloured locks hung limp, refusing to take on even the slightest hint of curl even in the dry climate of home. As she shampooed, she feared the humidity here might drive her hair and herself to madness far sooner than the problems with her property.

*

Zara pushed the button for the elevator. Wearing black slacks, a sleeveless white collared shirt and a wide black patent belt, she looked sufficiently trade-certified for her meeting this morning. As feared, her hair turned out a limp mess and she pinned it up with a large clip. A pair of chic-framed reading glasses completed the business ensemble.

Waiting, her eyes focused on the gigantic urn set on the floor between the two elevator doors. At least four feet tall and constructed from glossy green marble, a spearlike bundle of flowers and grasses protruded from it. *It's all about scale,* Zara thought, noting how the large arrangement commanded the rectangular space in the elevator foyer. The kinds of things a trained designer and architect would notice. The doors opened and clutching her shiny red Fendi bag that doubled as purse and briefcase, she stepped inside.

She pushed the button for the ground floor, then remembered the conference rooms were on the mezzanine level, so pushed that button as well. The elevator came to a stop on the fourth floor.

The doors opened, but she didn't see anyone. As they began to close, a hand slammed between them forcing them to retract again. Zara jumped at the sudden movement, saw the flex of a man's arm and the connecting body come into view. Except for the hotel towel loosely covering his lower body, he was naked.

The man hopped into the elevator and whirled around to look out the doors, as if evading a pursuer. Zara stared at his nude bottom right there in front of her. A great-looking one, too--rivalling some she'd seen on Ladies' night at the Cove Club in Montreal. Still wet, probably having come from the pool or showers, droplets of water coalesced on his skin and ran in streams down his body and onto the floor.

Embarrassed, she turned her face to the wall, but couldn't quite stifle a giggle. As the elevator doors eased shut he turned to face her, suddenly aware of her presence and clutched the towel with both hands.

"Senorita, lo siento," he said. "But I must get away from them..." He tipped his head toward the doors, as if indicating a mob that chased him. Extraordinarily handsome, his dark hair fell wet and dripping over his forehead.

Then he shook his head like a dog, spraying her with water. She flinched and wiped her face with the back of her hand. "Oh, lo siento," he said again in a desperate voice. He started to offer her the towel, but as she let out a short scream and put her hands over her eyes, he quickly covered himself again.

The elevator reached the mezzanine and Zara edged her way past him to the doors, shielding him from view with one hand. The man started to laugh. "Verdad, I am okay, really Senorita, I'm not dangerous…"

"No hay problema," she stammered, stepping out onto the mezzanine. As she moved away, she heard him laugh again and shout, "What are you doing Tuesday night?" The metallic thud of the elevator doors cut off his voice.

She stumbled across the marble floor of the mezzanine, grabbing onto the metal railing overlooking the lobby. *Who the hell was that?* And where exactly did he think he would get away to, stark naked and riding an elevator on its way down to the lobby? The people waiting for the lift were in for a big surprise.

As she looked around for the hallway leading to the conference rooms, she heard screams coming from below and laughed out loud.

CHAPTER THREE

Ernesto laid his briefcase on the conference room table and began to open it when a large, balding man entered the room, making wide gestures and talking loudly in Spanish to the man following behind him. He greeted Ernesto with a hearty "Buenas días, old friend. Good to see you again." Ernesto looked up, pushing his eyeglasses into position and nodding.

"Buenas días, Ignacio. I'll agree with the friend part, but hopefully not the old," Ernesto said with a light chuckle.

As the Planning and Development officer for the region, Ignacio Verrera was an irritating but necessary addition to the meeting personnel. Ernesto had dealt with him more times than he cared to remember. Verrera had every project in the area under his direction in one way or another. A good businessman for the most part, he stood out of the way of progress and the potential for tourism dollars flowing into the Costa del Sol. But too talkative, in Ernesto's opinion. The man rambled incessantly, about everything and nothing. And he had a slimy way about him, always leaving Ernesto with the impression he'd just been in the presence of a talking reptile.

"I am told El Mirador has a new owner," Verrera said, shaking hands with Ernesto and seating himself at the conference table. "This is Bernardo, my assistant," he added, introducing the man who accompanied him. Ernesto shook his hand. Verrera should have been a politician, Ernesto thought. He had the demeanour and trappings of one, including a sidekick--this Bernardo character.

"Miss Zara Flynn, from Montreal," Ernesto confirmed. He returned to his briefcase, digging out file folders, a pen, his Smartphone.

"Flynn?" repeated Verrera. "As in Flynn Enterprises?"

"Si, the heiress herself, I suppose you might call her. Tristan's daughter. She's expected shortly," Ernesto said and nodded towards the door.

Verrera checked his watch. "Not still on American time, I hope?" He grinned.

"Canadian, actually," Ernesto said. "Not the same at all."

Verrera scoffed. "You're a funny man, Alvarez. American, Canadian. They both eat too much beef and drink the wrong wine with dinner." He chuckled outright, turning to Bernardo and encouraging him to join in the joke.

Annoyed, Ernesto peered over the top of his glasses at Verrera. It wasn't important what Verrera thought of Miss Flynn, but it would help if he had some measure of respect for her since she held the deed to the property they were about to discuss.

"Thank you, Ignacio. I'm sure she'll take that as a compliment."

With a dismissive wave, Verrera turned back to Bernardo and began a conversation in Spanish. A slight, unremarkable-looking man with his hair shaved short, Bernardo wore a shirt and tie with a v-neck pullover vest. He seemed focused on Verrera's dialogue, but not particularly interested.

Ernesto glanced toward the door, wondering when Zara would make her entrance. He almost felt nervous. He hadn't seen her since she'd been a young girl, but heard Tristan talk of her many times, the pride in his daughter evident. Her excellent grades in school, her spunk at refusing to take the easy route and accept a position with Flynn Enterprises. He hoped she was equal to the task ahead at El Mirador. Her father had certainly thought so.

The door to the conference room swung open and Ernesto felt a lump in his throat as Zara walked in. *She looks so much like her mother.* "Senorita Flynn," he finally said after an awkward pause, extending his arm as if to scoop her off the threshold and into the room. "Welcome, did you have a pleasant flight?"

"Yes, thank you," Zara said, stepping forward and nodding to the two other men. She reserved a warm smile for Alvarez. "How good to see you, Ernesto. I remember you at my parents' anniversary party."

Ernesto laughed. "My, that was many years ago. You weren't more than thirteen or fourteen then."

Zara nodded in agreement. "I have a good memory. My mother and father talked of you often."

Ernesto returned a grateful smile. Her remark reminded him what a great loss they'd all suffered with the death of a man like Tristan Flynn. "I'm honoured. It's wonderful to see you as well."

Ernesto began the introductions. "Miss Zara Flynn, this is Ignacio Verrera, chief development officer with the regional government and his assistant, Sr. Bernardo..." Ernesto paused, waiting for the man to volunteer his surname. He stood with his hands in his pockets.

"Cruz," he said, suddenly lifting his right hand from his pants pocket and extending it to Zara. "Bernardo Cruz," he finished. They shook hands, and Verrera followed suit, instead taking Zara's hand in his palm and raising it to his lips.

"Senorita," he said with admiration, "what a pleasure to meet you. I trust you are enjoying your stay so far?" He stared into her eyes, as though waiting for an answer before releasing her hand.

"So far," Zara said. "Which hasn't been long."

Verrera smiled in acknowledgement. "All in good time, then," he said, finally letting go. As if to wipe away his sweaty touch, Zara brushed her hand on her slacks and moved towards a swivel chair at the head of the table, near Ernesto. He pulled the chair out and when she'd been seated, motioned for the others to sit before taking the chair next to her.

"So you have seen El Mirador, Miss Flynn?" Ernesto said, placing a set of architectural renderings on the table in front of her. Quite taken by her appearance, he remembered Marlena as a young woman and her daughter bore a striking resemblance. An old wound began to re-open in Ernesto's heart. *That was a long time ago*, he reminded himself.

Zara reviewed the drawings, the cover page showing a finished exterior view, complete with sunbathers and beach umbrellas in the foreground and parasailers in the blue sky above.

El Mirador. The Viewpoint, or vantage point, as it meant in English.

"I saw it on the way from the airport." She held up the drawing. "Are these the restoration proposals?"

Verrera spoke. "These plans were approved by my office six months ago, Senorita Flynn. Unfortunately, the project has been delayed due to certain...circumstances." She turned to Ernesto, who looked down at his papers on the table.

"What circumstances?"

Ernesto handed her copies of the fax he'd received. Sent from Vistamar Holdings, the first page described the site as an 'extreme ecological hazard,' with 'Methane and H2S gas present. Foundation considered unstable due to marshy substrate.' The existing structure had been deemed 'unsafe' and demolition was advised.

An offer to purchase filled the second page, for 1.25 million Euro, about 25 percent of Flynn's original purchase price of five million. Small change, by comparison.

Ernesto felt pity at her crestfallen look. "I know it is not what you hoped," he said. "But before we do anything, we should complete our own inspection of the site. Please don't visit there again without official escort and proper safety wear, you promise?"

Zara sighed. "Yes, yes, Ernesto, I promise." She gave him an assuring glance, like a good student deferring to the teacher's authority. Ernesto nodded and laid the fax sheets into his briefcase, closing it with a snap.

"What is Vistamar Holdings?" Zara asked.

"A relatively new company," Verrera answered. "Subcontractors. The municipality has used them to do survey work, generally on public and state lands. They specialize in health and safety assessments."

Ernesto coughed into his fist. "Verdad, that's true. But they also specialize in reclamation," he said in a flat tone. "Which is, I assume, why they are interested in acquisition."

"Who ordered this assessment?" Zara asked.

Again, Verrera interjected. "It is...protocolo, for any government lands, he said. "Waterfront is ordinarily state property. A private sale is unusual." An ingratiating smile creased his round face. "Sr. Flynn was very influential."

His attempt at a compliment appeared to give Zara a chill. "Why has the site not been redeveloped before now? she asked, her voice icy.

Verrera's smile faded to a look of mild condescension. "Well," he said, tilting his head toward her. "Things here do not move as quickly as they might where you have come from, Senorita."

Zara regarded him skeptically.

Ernesto sensed her growing annoyance and decided to cut

the meeting short. "That's all for today, gentlemen," he said. "Thank you for coming, we will be in touch."

Verrera seemed surprised at Alvarez' sudden dismissal. He glanced over at Cruz, but shrugged and said, "Very well. You can reach us at my office." Verrera stood and nodded to Zara. "Senorita," he said and turned to leave. Cruz followed him out.

Ernesto watched them go, then turned to Zara. "I've arranged for someone from our office to lead the site inspection on Wednesday. Why don't you go and have lunch now and I'll confirm the time with you before you finish a Spanish coffee."

"Thank you, Ernesto." She nodded toward the door. "Rather odd...that Sr. Cruz, didn't you think?" She paused, looking thoughtful. "You knew my father a long time. I trust you. It doesn't seem like you trust *them*." She gestured after the two men. "I can't believe El Mirador's just been left to rot all these years. Did my father discuss his intentions with you when he bought it? Or his long-term plans for it?"

Ernesto drew a long breath and ran his hand over the leather surface of his briefcase while considering his answer. There was more to his relationship with Tristan than she knew. He thought he had put his feelings behind him when he had relinquished Marlena, his childhood sweetheart, to his friend Tristan. The better man, who had won her heart.

"Not in detail," he said. "I didn't question your father's motives, but of course we discussed his initial ideas about the restoration--how it should look, what structural concerns he had and so forth. I ordered the concept renderings you are holding at his request." Ernesto sighed before continuing. "But no, I didn't have a chance to talk with him much since. I wasn't one of the last people to see him before he died; I'm sure you would like some insight into his last words, thoughts. I'm sorry. I haven't any for you. I wish I did."

"When did you see him last?"

"About a month before he left for Jakarta, where…the accident happened." Ernesto gave himself a mental kick. *She already knew that, estupid.* "He intended to go in September but…he went early.*"*

"Who was with him?"

"Mostly the local workforce," he said. "Some of them were lost in the explosion also," he reminded her, hoping her compassion for others would help keep things in perspective.

She closed her eyes, furrowing her brow. "There must have been a foreman present? A supervisor or crew chief at least?"

"Zara," he said, his voice quiet with understanding. "Of course you want answers. We all do, but the Javanese government is making access to information difficult. It happened after hours. Your father and the others were," he paused. "…in the wrong place at the wrong time."

Even as he spoke them, Ernesto knew these were unsatisfying words, that didn't qualify as explanation. Silent for a moment, Zara appeared unable to think of anything else except to change the subject.

"I'll be in Marbella for a few weeks, before I go to Zaragoza," she said firmly. "I want to contribute to the company while I'm here. What is the office address?" Ernesto reached into his jacket pocket for a business card. Taking out a pen, he wrote on the reverse side before handing it to her.

"The address and telephone numbers are on the card, but here are my home and cell phone numbers. Don't hesitate to call if you have any other questions. Why don't you come to the office after the site visit. Perhaps Thursday?"

He smiled and touched her shoulder in a fatherly gesture. He wanted to help her any way he could. As Marlena's flesh and blood, she was precious to him. "We must bring Tristan's vision to life, si? Don't worry, it will be magnifico."

Zara smiled back. "Si. Magnifico!"

CHAPTER FOUR

Zara spotted Jorge reading a newspaper in the terrace café. She ducked under the archway leading to the sunny outdoor space and made her way towards him.

"Buenas días, Jorge," she said, sliding into the seat next to him. "What's good on the menu, I'm starved."

Jorge let the top half of his newspaper flap down to look at her.

"Everything is good here; the lunch menu is always, as you say, 'a big deal' in Espana." He moved his coffee cup aside to make space at the tile-topped table.

Zara smiled. She remembered this from her last visit. Breakfast here consisted of not much more than coffee and a churro in anticipation of lunchtime. The locals started preparing the next day's lunch almost as soon as they finished today's. Lasting until perhaps two p.m., most everything would shut down until six or seven. Heaven help you if you were hungry before nine p.m., but booze…no problem. Beer was cheaper than water here, or even Coke. The Spanish liked to stay out late--often partying until dawn. No wonder caffeine and pastry were all anyone could stomach in the morning, she mused. Best get while the getting was good.

She perused the menu.

After ordering a light seafood dish and glass of white wine, she took her Blackberry from the Fendi bag and checked for messages. Her mother must have texted her by now. Yup. *Land safe? How is weather, Jorge taking good care of u? Call me when you're settled, luv u.* Zara replied that all was well and would text back later. She slipped the phone back into its pocket.

"How was your meeting, Miss? Jorge asked. Did you find out much about El Mirador?"

"Yes," she said with a sigh. "And no." *I found out there are naked men running around this hotel, though.* She smirked in recollection. It was looking like the highlight of her day so far. "Had you seen it before, Jorge? Before yesterday?"

Jorge shook his head, folded his paper and rose from the table, as if deliberately ignoring the question. "I am off to see my sister and her family for the afternoon, Miss. Is there anything you need before I go?"

The server approached with Zara's lunch. She shook her head.

"Thank you Jorge, I'm still a bit jet-lagged. I just need to relax for a while. Please say hi to Elena and the girls for me."

"Si, lo haré. I will return this evening, but...perhaps you would like to come along?" he asked, as an afterthought. He seemed hesitant to leave her alone on her first day.

Zara picked up her glass of wine from the table. "No, but thank you for asking. You have a nice visit, I'm sure they're looking forward to seeing you."

Jorge donned his hat and strode away.

She sipped her wine and taking a deep breath, paused to admire the garden foliage surrounding the terrace. *So beautiful.* She wished she could enjoy it more, but after the news from the meeting she felt on edge. And more than a little nervous about the site visit.

Aside from Alvarez, she didn't know any of her father's business associates here. What would they think of her, a 24-year old rookie fresh out of architecture school waltzing in to try to run the business? Expecting her to make decisions and answer questions. She wasn't inexperienced, but far from an expert in corporate matters.

She took another sip of wine and started in on her fish. As she ate, she heard a woman's brash voice coming from around a potted plant a few tables away.

"Wot, wi' this heat?" The woman spoke with a northern British accent. "On yer bike wi' ya. Bring me a G and T, luv." Zara looked over to see a slim, older gentleman shuffle out from behind the plant and make his way toward the bar. "And some of them tapas, too, Diggy."

The man muttered in response. "Yes, yes luv, I've 'eard you." Diggy's route steered by Zara's table. He spotted her and smiled. "What wifey wants, wifey gets!" he said and sent her a friendly wink. She watched him get a round of drinks from the bar and as he shuffled back past Zara's table, he placed a second glass of white wine next to her first.

"Young lady all on her own, eh? Well, enjoy another drink on old Diggy won't you?" he said when she looked up at him in surprise.

"Who's that you're talking to, Dig?" Zara heard the woman say.

"Just a lass needing a bit of refreshment, luv," he responded, making his return around the potted plant. "Nice-looking too, she'd best not be left on her own I say."

Zara rolled her eyes.

"Well, why the hell didn't you invite her to join us, you absent-minded git."

Zara picked up the glass of wine Diggy had brought and followed his path around the plant to introduce herself.

"Excuse me," Zara said and the couple turned to look at her

simultaneously. "Thank you for the wine. You're quite right; I am all on my own more or less." She looked at the woman and smiled. Large, middle-aged, heavy set with bleached-blond hair teased up in a coarse beehive on the top of her head. Short tendrils of curly hair that wouldn't fit in the beehive framed her face. She wore a bright floral-patterned blouse with a deep v-neck that showed off her ample cleavage. "Your husband is very kind."

"Well then," the woman said, slapping her hand on the table. "You must join us. Diggy, pull up a chair!" She made a swooping gesture at him with a pointy, pink gel fingernail. The shade matched her overdone lipstick.

"Bette Ridley," she said, thrusting out a hand to Zara. "This here's Diggy, the love-o-me-life."

Diggy nodded and smiled, as he pulled one of the wrought-iron chairs over to their table.

"Oh, I don't mean to intrude, really." She shook Bette's outstretched hand. "I just wanted to say thanks. I should be going, I've a lot of work to do," Zara said, taking a step backward--only to bump into the chair Diggy had already placed behind her legs.

"Rubbish!" Bette said. "Work! Who comes here to work? You're on the beach girl, have a seat and another drink. Fancy sommat stronger than that wine, like a G and T?"

Zara sat as commanded. Bette was not the kind of woman you said no to.

"This is fine," Zara said, brandishing her wineglass. Zara hadn't anything that pressing after all and really could use some diversion. The couple seemed very familiar with the place. Perhaps she could ask them a few questions.

"What's you're name then, luv?"

"Zara...Zara Flynn. Do the two of you come here often?"

Bette and Diggy exchanged wry glances. "Oh yes, luv. Nigh twenty years now, ain't it Dig?"

"Too right, luv. Twenty and then some, I expect," Diggy said, raising his pint glass.

"We fancy the weather here in Spain, like most folks from our neck of the woods. Mind you, not always been the Marbella, we've been all over this lot. Ibiza, Tenerife, Tangiers too. It's right upscale here though, we like it," Bette said.

"Where are you two from, then?" Zara asked.

"Egad lass, we's from Liverpool, like most Brits what come here," Bette said, swigging her gin and tonic with a flourish. "Paella's fine but," she leaned in a little closer, "I like to find a decent chippy, y'know…sometimes it's comfort foods you fancy, eh?" Another swig of gin. "You're from America, yeah?"

Zara took another sip of wine. "Do I seem American?" she asked innocently, always curious why anyone with a western accent was immediately assumed to be American. She noticed it often on her travels.

"Well, aren't you, globe-trotting on your own, fancy designer bag and all?"

"I live in Montreal, but I was born in Ontario," Zara said, wondering what kind of reaction they'd have.

"Ah," Diggy said and brightened, cutting in between his wife's chattering. "You're from Canada then." He nodded and smiled. "Great country. Loyal to Her Majesty, bless them."

"Yes, yes," Bette said. "Royal watchers they are, follow the tabs on the Royal family."

"So, you've stayed at Club Marbella before?" Zara steered the conversation back on track. "Which airport did you fly in to?"

"Charter from Heathrow into Malaga this time," Bette said. "And you?"

"Seville." Zara said. "I passed by something on the coast road on the way here. An old building, called El Mirador. Have you heard of it?"

Bette raised her eyebrows. "Ohh, yes luv, I've heard of it--and the stories 'round it, too."

"Stories? Really--like what?"

"Well," Bette said, glancing left and right as if she didn't want to be overheard. "They say a woman and her lover burned to death in it. Torched it was, struck by lightning I think." She looked over at Diggy, oblivious as he swilled his pint. "Dig, pay attention!" Bette snapped. "Lightning, wasn't it?"

"Naw," Diggy said, licking the foam from his lips. "Pirates, I heard."

Bette snorted. "Pirates…what are you on about, you silly mug. Lightning," she repeated, nodding with finality.

Diggy snapped his fingers. "Oh wait--now I remember--'twas ghosts of Moorish sailors, avenging their conquest by the Spaniards. Sent flaming arrows from a ghost ship out at sea. Phoosh!" He raised his arms in an exploding gesture. Then he winked.

Zara smiled and looked down at her lap. *No help here.*

"Pay him no mind, luv," Bette said. "Pirates…" she muttered, rolling her eyes and shaking her head. "I tell you, a woman died there. That much is true."

At least they agreed on the fire, Zara thought. Maybe another tack. "Did you see anything… unusual…this morning?"

Bette downed the last of her G and T. "Unusual? Like what?" she asked.

"Unusual say, a naked man running from the spa to the elevator, for example?"

Bette nearly spit out her gin.

"Say what? Naked man? I wish to God I had, missy! Ha!" Lowering her voice, she added, "Was he a looker, or just an old punter who lost his way to the loo?"

"Oh, he was quite good-looking," Zara said. "So was his butt."

Bette's cheeks glowed pink on either side of her excited

grin. "Why the hell didn't you chase him down, then? You let him get away!"

"I take it it's not unusual, then," Zara concluded.

Bette raised her eyebrows. "We're on the beach in Spain, dear...wouldn't be normal without naked men around, or women and all!"

The server made an appearance just then, clearing their lunch plates and taking another order of drinks. "Another round, sweetheart, and one for yourself," Diggy said to the girl, hoisting his empty pint mug toward her.

"Well, I really should be going," Zara said, pushing her chair back from the little table.

"Aww, we was just getting to know you, luv...please stay."

"I promise I'll have a drink with you another time. Thank you for a lovely conversation."

Bette called out as Zara moved away. "Come to the stage show tomorrow night, dear...sit with us."

"What's playing?"

"Don't you know? Bloody hell, it's only Mickey Mountain!" Bette said. "Miguel Montana, dear," she added, seeing Zara's blank look. "Eight o'clock."

Miguel. Where had she heard that name?

CHAPTER FIVE

It felt good on her face, the brilliant, unfailing Mediterranean sun. It warmed her chest, her thighs and the backs of her hands. Zara knew she should have covered her head or worn a hat of some kind, but screw it. Back in Montreal Old Man Winter would be nipping at her heels. She'd take the sunshine as much as she wanted here and now.

She'd removed her bikini top. It dangled lazily over the back of her deck chair. The hot rays felt delicious on her bare breasts. *When in Rome,* she thought. *Or Spain.* The Mediterranean sun-seekers had no compunctions about removing their clothing, so why should she? *Five more minutes, then I'll start back to my room and get ready for tonight.*

Rested, her internal clock had finally reset itself. She'd spent most of the day lazing around the resort, venturing down to the fourth floor to use the workout room and whirlpool without running in to any stray, naked men. She swam in the pools, walked around the gardens, read a book and sipped Perrier at will. Now she lay on a deck chair on the beach.

If there was any place closer to heaven, Zara couldn't think of it.

Reluctantly she reached for her top and put it back on. Gathering her belongings and stuffing them into the shiny red bag, she departed from the beach and walked the stone path back to the resort. She found a message waiting for her at the desk from Bette and Diggy inviting her to meet them for dinner at the *Paraiso* dining room before attending the stage show.

She pawed through the clothes she'd hung in the closet, selecting a red silk dress and silver strappy sandals. She slipped the dress on, flipped her hair back over her shoulders and examined herself in the mirror. The silk had a darker red floral pattern to it and the deep-cut halter style top criss-crossed in the back. Turning to look at herself from the rear, she smiled at the way the design showed off her shoulder blades.

The dress looked great, but her hair...well. *Damn this humidity.* She'd managed to ignore it most of the day by wearing it up. Now she desperately needed to make her hair look acceptable for a dinner date somehow.

She plugged in her hot rollers. Starting by brushing it with her head down, she applied a few palmfuls of mousse to her dry hair for some extra muscle. A quick shot with the blow dryer and when the rollers were ready, she sectioned her locks and wound them around the biggest ones, re-applying her makeup while they set.

Searching though the bottles on the bathroom vanity she found the Paloma Picasso and spritzed it on the front and back of her neck, both wrists and behind her knees.

Removing the rollers, she gave the curls a comb through and a finishing spritz of extreme-hold hair spray. Buckling the skinny ankle straps of her high-heeled silver sandals, she grabbed her trusty red bag and breezed out the door.

*

Situated on the inland side of the hotel, the *Paraiso* dining room afforded tranquil views of the hills to the north. Greenery and the fresh scent of flowers pervaded the indoor space and extended out onto to a long balcony. As dusk fell, thousands of mini-lights illuminated the walls and bejewelled the shrubs bordering the balcony.

Zara saw Bette and Diggy waving to her as she entered. The dining room host escorted her to their table and pulled out a chair.

"Aww, don't you look a picture," Bette said, her voice a dovelike coo. "No more Miss Business tonight!"

Diggy stood and nodded his approval.

"You look lovely, dear."

"Thank you," Zara said with a smile and ordered a lime margarita. "I feel lovely. I had a great day all to myself. Something I don't get very often."

Bette smiled. "You deserve it, luv. And it shows...such a lovely frock."

The three of them ate happily, exchanging stories and toasting drinks. Bette revealed that she and Diggy owned a curiosity shop back in Liverpool, consigning everything from teapots to trading cards. Diggy had been in the army and enjoyed a comfortable service pension while entertaining his skeet-shooting hobby and keeping the shop running.

Before long it was show time, and the three made their way to the adjoining theatre for the evening concert. The lush, padded auditorium smelled lightly of lemons and roses, the air circulating in refreshing waves from the overhead fans.

"I can't believe you've not heard of Miguel Montana," Bette said as they settled in their seats. "He's only one of the hottest acts on the continent right now."

"What are some of his songs?" Zara asked, more interested in observing the sweeping curve of the balcony structure and rococo-esque, pastel décor of the space than in Montana's repertoire.

"Oh, there's loads," Bette said as the lights began to dim. The rest of her words drowned in the overture music that rose from the stage pit. A tangible anticipation swelled in the room.

The emcee announced, first in Spanish then in English, "Ladies and Gentlemen, please welcome Spain's very own international singing star, Miguel Montana!"

The intro music grew louder, the audience swayed and clapped to the beat. Zara could feel an accelerating energy in the air. The curtains parted and her breath caught as dancers literally exploded onto the front of the stage, live fireworks igniting behind them as they leapt forward. Stunning girls and buff young men in sequined outfits whirled and moved to the music before pairing off, creating an entranceway for the headliner at center stage.

Excitement rippled through her as the sharp ozone residue tickled her nostrils and a riser at the back of the stage brought a silhouetted figure into view. The figure struck a pose, an arm raised pointing toward the stars on the backdrop.

The theatre erupted in screams as the spotlight hit the stage and he turned his face to the audience. The star rotated his arm forward to point directly at the crowd and advanced to centre stage, his athletic body moving seductively to the pounding Latin rhythm.

He dressed in white leather pants and a matching sleeveless tunic cut in a low V at the neck, with loose laces criss-crossing his bronzed, sculpted chest. Grabbing the microphone, he belted out his opening song, eliciting even louder screams from the largely female audience.

Holy shit, Zara thought, *this guy's big news around here*. Her jaw dropped as she watched his magnificent physique writhing sexily on stage, his appeal further heightened by the tight leather suit and the soul-ripping power of his voice. He strutted stage right, towards where she and the Ridleys sat.

Mesmerized, Zara watched him as he drew to the very edge

of the stage in front of them. Her eyes followed the length of his body from his feet to his thighs, lingering a moment at his crotch, then past his waist and upward to his chest and neck. Framed by dark hair expertly gelled into place, she saw his face in startling clarity and something flipped over in her stomach.

Oh God, she knew this guy...he was the naked elevator man.

She raised her hand to her mouth, a burning sensation rising in her cheeks. The ceiling fans might as well have been nonexistent as she felt the air grow hot around her. The singer kept moving to the right, the bright stage lights reflecting off his white outfit and the Spanish lyrics flowing way too fast for Zara to catch any of the words.

He continued to sing with punctuating gestures to the audience, until he looked directly at her. *He couldn't possibly see me with the stage lights on,* she thought. Yet he seemed to point straight at her, tilting his head to one side, a flirtatious smirk playing on his face as he continued with his song. Reversing his steps he moved stage left, acknowledging the fans on the other side of the theater.

A group of girls swarmed to the front of the stage, reaching out to the sexy star. Miguel kept singing, smiling wide as he reached down to touch some of the outstretched hands at his feet. He retreated to centre stage, replaced the microphone on its stand and started in on a solo dance routine. The stage dancers spun and gyrated around him. But as good as they were, she couldn't take her eyes off the star of the show.

Intense and hypnotizing, his movements practically spelled the word *sex*. For a nanosecond, she actually thought she *smelled* sex. Zara shifted in her seat, partly to get a better look at him but mostly to interrupt the feelings of arousal stirring within her.

His thousand-watt smile seemed even more brilliant in

contrast to his bronze skin and shadow of dark beard on his chiselled jaw. *Gorgeous,* Zara thought as she continued to stare at him, wondering what rock she'd been under to have never heard of this entertainer before. *Drop-effing-dead gorgeous.*

The opening number ended and the dancers landed in a crouch surrounding Miguel who stood tall in the centre of the circle. He hit the final note while raising his hands in an almost saintly pose. He stood still in the spotlight, breathing heavily and basking in the applause of the audience. Then he lowered his arms and took a deep bow. Straightening, he waved and shouted '*Gracias!*'

The lighting changed, shifting from white spotlight to a fluttering aurora of color. The dancers moved apart and Miguel turned away from the audience and marched to the back of the stage. Zara watched the marvellously sculpted butt she had just seen in its natural state a day ago swing seductively away from her. The orchestra segued into the next number and the dancers regrouped in the front of the stage.

Bette slapped a hand on Zara's arm, the applause still thundering from the opening song. "Wasn't that brilliant!" she exclaimed, doing a quick double take upon seeing Zara's face. "Dearie, are you alright? You look as though you've seen a ghost!"

Zara clasped Bette's hand and leaned in to speak in her ear. "That's the naked man I told you about."

CHAPTER SIX

Bette sat next to Zara at a tall table in the late-night bar, sliding a gin and tonic towards her and insisting she drink it down. "What a shock, eh? I must say girl, I'm right jealous of you. You've seen Mickey Mountain with his kit off! How many can say that, eh? C'mon, get that down you!"

With the events of the last few days and perhaps a little too much sun, Zara was well past caring how much alcohol she'd consumed. She took a big swallow from the glass in front of her.

"Does the body live up to the name, then?" Bette asked.

It was Zara's turn to nearly spit out her drink, as she caught Bette's joke. "Can't say. He had his…meat and vegetables… covered with a towel," she said. Bette squealed with laughter.

Why didn't I catch on right away? Zara thought. It all made sense, now. Despite his best efforts, he he'd probably been spotted on the fourth floor by some of his fans and had to make tracks out of the spa. The getaway car just happened to be her elevator.

She took another gulp of her gin, saw Bette wave to the server to bring another round. Diggy sat at the bar a discreet distance from the two women, apparently content to give them a little girl time. He nursed his usual pint of beer, chatting with the bartender.

The cocktails kept coming until last call. Zara felt barely able to hold her head steady. "Oh, shit," she said, looking at her watch. "I gotta get up in the morning; I have a site visit at ten." She hiccupped, and then clapped her hand to her mouth.

Bette laughed at her. "Best get you off to bed then, lass. C'mon," she said matter-of-factly and climbed down off her barstool to take Zara by the arm. "Dig. Let's go, luv--time for nighty-night." Diggy polished off his last pint, said a few words to the barkeep and came over to help.

"I'm fine, really," Zara said. "No need, I can see myself out."

"Shush, girl," Bette said as she and Diggy guided her across the room towards the exit. Before they made it to the hallway, a duo of gentlemen approached. One a bit taller than the other, they both wore dark suits and bluetooth earpieces.

"Perdoneme," the taller one said, "we don't mean to frighten you. We have a message for...Miss Red Dress." He gestured at Zara. She looked up, blinking, then straightened to her full height, a smug look pasted on her face.

"What message, we're escorting her to her room now. It's late, gents," Diggy said, trying to warn them off.

"Lo siento, Senorita," continued the taller dark suit, looking like a cross between James Bond and Agent Smith. "It is late, but our employer wishes to invite you to a...private party. It's very important that we take you there." He held out his hand. "Por favor, Miss."

Zara swayed a little, supported on either side by her adopted English guardians and broke out in a naughty grin. "In that case, I accept."

Bette snorted and gripped her arm tighter. "No you're not, lassie; you know you shouldn't talk to strangers, and this lot's the strangest I've seen in awhile."

"It's my party and I'll spy if I want to," she giggled, jerking her arm away and stepping forward. "Lead on, double-oh-seven." The men now replaced Bette and Diggy on either side of her, leaving the couple behind as they swept her toward the elevators.

"Mind your p's and q's luv!" Bette called after her.

"Who's throwing this party, then?" Zara asked, looking from one dark suit to the other as the elevator rose skyward.

"A surpresa, Senorita. We are certain you'll be pleased with your host." They stood with their hands behind their backs, not saying any more. Zara sniffed and watched the floor numbers light up one by one as they ascended, trying not to let a spinning sensation take over her from the several gin and tonics she'd drank. The number 12 illuminated, then a letter P, where the elevator slowed to a stop.

A panoramic view of the sea greeted them as they stepped out onto the penthouse level. Starry skies and moonlit breakers shimmered through the wall of windows in front of them. The dark suits turned left and escorted her to the one and only door at the end of the hall. The shorter dark suit swiped his cardkey in the electronic lock and swung the door wide, motioning Zara to enter.

In the dimly lit room, she heard soft guitar music. She took a few steps forward and the suits backed out into the hallway and closed the door, not accompanying her further.

Zara whirled around as the door made an ominous click. She banged her hands against it.

"Hey, what do you think you're doing," she shouted. The door handle didn't budge as she pushed down on it. Panic wavered at the edges of her brain. *Doors don't lock from the outside.*

Didn't seem like much of a party going either--she appeared to be alone. But then the suits did say 'private party'....*Shit.* Why did she leave the bar with those goons? *Stupid, stupid, girl.*

She stood still in the vestibule, checking her surroundings.
The music had a soothing effect on her gin-addled brain. Tiny
pin lights in the ceiling around the perimeter of the room
ahead sparkled softly. A pleasant scent filled the air. *She had
to do something. Think.* She dug for the cell phone in her bag,
fumbling with its contents.

"Entrez, mademoiselle robe rouge," she heard a man's
voice call. In French.

"Que est?" Zara said with what she hoped sounded like
authority, her hand frozen around her Blackberry. He stepped
out from around the corner just a foot or so ahead of her,
reaching out to clasp her wrist.

"C'est moi, mademoiselle," he said, drawing her close.

Even with his face in shadow, she recognized Miguel.
Showered, shaved and dressed in something, ah, much more
comfortable than his white leather outfit of earlier. "Did you
apprécier la performance?" he asked in a quiet voice.

Dumbstruck, Zara could do nothing but stare at him. *I'm in
freaking Miguel Montana's hotel room.* Her mind went fuzzy.
She should not have come--yet now wanted to stay. He had
his hand entwined with hers so that their forearms met from
wrist to elbow and they stood chest to chest. He wore a spicy,
sensual cologne.

"Oui, c'est formidable," she answered. "But you had better
let me out of this room right now before I…"

He interrupted by pressing a finger against her lips. "I
am sorry to…sneak you here, mademoiselle. Please don't be
angry. Won't you visit with me for awhile, let me apologize
for embarrassing you yesterday."

"I wasn't embarrassed--you were the one with no clothes
on," she said.

He smiled and removed his finger from her lips. "C'est
vrai, I was. And I am sorry. I owe you an explanation."

"I accept your apology, you don't need to explain--your

fans tonight did it for you. But you should let me go now. I'm not feeling well."

He looked sincerely worried. "Then you must stay," he said. "I'll make you feel better…I'm very good at that. Please stay. Aren't you wondering how I found you?"

Zara swayed a little, her resolve crumbling. He looked so vulnerable--his brown eyes brimming wide and pleading like a cocker spaniel. She had no doubt he was good at making women feel better.

"I saw you in the audience," Miguel said. "But I began my research the minute you stepped off the elevator."

"Research? How do you mean?" she asked.

"I have many friends traveling with me who find things out when I ask. You parler Francais, then? I only made a guess when I learned you were from Montreal."

"Naturellement," she answered. "But most people from my country learn at least a little French. If only from reading the back side of a cereal box."

Miguel laughed softly. "I knew you would have a sense of humour. You were very funny when I surprised you in my towel." He stared into her eyes. "Ah," he said suddenly and switched to Spanish. "Por favor, please come in, sit. May I offer you something to drink?"

Zara almost hiccupped, but stifled it and realized she'd had quite enough to drink already. "Perhaps some water?" he suggested. Then he smiled and nodded. "Si, agua. You won't mind if I open some champagne?"

Zara shook her head slowly, taking a serious look at him, all of him. He wore a plain pair of beige khakis but no shirt. Her gaze panned over his well-defined abs, arms, hands and his bare feet on the marble tiles of the floor. The most perfect male feet she'd ever seen. *Whoa, wait a sec.* Were his toenails…*painted?* She blinked, not entirely trusting her eyesight under the circumstances.

He led her to a fabulous black leather couch in the greatroom and sat her down. "Don't go away," he said, moving off to the galley kitchen.

The room was huge compared to her suite and the furnishings more luxurious. The pin lighting cast a glittering yet relaxing ambience to the room. Fatigue began to set in and she sank back into the comfortable couch, going over the architectural details of the place in her mind, never quite able to shut the designer engine off completely.

Miguel returned with three glasses, one of water and two of champagne. "In case you change your mind," he said, setting all three on the coffee table in front of her and offering her the water glass.

"Gracias," she said and sipped it down to help clear her head and ward off tomorrow's hangover. The liquid had the distinctive tang of mineral water. He sat next to her and toasted his glass to hers.

"Thank you for coming." He seemed a perfect gentleman; Zara tried to keep her guard up but felt her eyelids begin to droop.

"I didn't have that much of a choice, thanks to your... boys." She put her glass down as if to leave. "I really shouldn't be here."

"Are you truly so disappointed?" he said, looking deeply into her eyes while taking a sip of his champagne.

"Well," she said, thinking it over. She wasn't exactly guiltless in the matter. "Not quite yet."

A clever smile crept across his handsome face as he set his glass down. "I am forgetting my manners," he said placing his hand on his chest. "My name is Miguel; I am honoured to meet you, Senorita. I, of course have already found out your name, but want to hear it from your own lovely lips. What is it?"

"My name is Zara Flynn, architect and as of yesterday,

CEO of Flynn Enterprises," she said with a flourish of her hand.

"Welcome Miss Flynn the architect, to my little universe for the evening," he said. "Smart as well as beautiful, I see. What will we build here tonight, do you think?"

She scanned his face at close range. A crooked, white scar snaked a route from the middle of his upper lip to just past his left nostril. *Aha. Not so perfect after all--stage makeup goes a long way.*

"Something unforgettable, I imagine."

Taking her hand, he rose from the couch, pulling her with him.

"Let me show you the universe." He led her to the penthouse windows that looked out onto the waterfront. Here the beach arched into a shallow cove, the lighted windows from neighbouring resorts reflecting off the water. Beyond that, the sparkling breakers of the Mediterranean appeared and disappeared against the blackness of the waves beneath them.

"This view is one of my favorites," he began. "You can see up the coastline almost all the way to Barcelona." They moved over to the bar where he said, "This is my bistro while I am touring and over here," he led her to the fireplace opposite the couch above which hung a large painting. "This is a portrait of my home. I have it placed in my hotel rooms so that home can still be with me when I am away from it so much."

The painting depicted a small harbour, with fishing boats tied to a pier and seabirds floating above. Silhouettes of pine forests covered the surrounding hills.

"It's lovely," she said. "Where is home?"

"San Sebastien. On the north coast, in Basque country. Yes, it is lovely," he agreed. "Like your name. Zara. Tell me how you came to have this name."

Zara smiled, thinking of her mother. "I was named after a place near here, where my mother was from."

Miguel's eyes lit up. "So you are partly Spanish, also? I should have known. Donde? Where?"

"Zaragoza. So she named me Zara."

He smiled, apparently delighted they had a shared heritage. They stood near the wall adjacent to the fireplace. He brought his palm up to her chin and turned her face towards him. Taking both her hands in his he pushed her gently but firmly towards the wall, flattening her against it.

Then he covered her mouth with his and she felt his hand trace down her thigh, finding the hem of her red silk skirt. He pushed it upwards until his hand met the curve of her buttocks. With her back to the wall, as the saying went, panic seeped back into her brain and her free hand rose to his chest in an attempt to resist. No good. Her muscles tingled and refused to work properly. Her eyes fell shut and she surrendered to the sweet pressure of his lips on hers.

Then the spinning sensation returned and everything went black.

CHAPTER SEVEN

What the hell was that noise? The ringing came again.
Zara's eyes slitted open as she unwillingly regained
consciousness and recognized the sound of the telephone. She
could make out the glowing red numbers on the clock. 9:18
a.m. Not daring to move her head, she reached for the phone
and brought it to the ear not covered by the pillow. She didn't
speak, but a familiar voice came over the receiver.

"Miss? It's after nine o'clock, we were to meet you at
nine...is everything all right?" Zara winced at the sound of
Jorge's voice as reality set in. She'd forgotten about the site
visit today. Oh God, she felt awful--her head pounded and
nausea rose in her throat.

"Jorge," she said, her voice croaky as a frog's. "I'm sorry,
can you give me 20 minutes? Are you in the lobby?"

"Si, Miss. There's a Sr. Parker with me. He is anxious to
get going. Do you need help, I can ask the concierge to send
someone up." Oh, she felt like a four year old, having to be
looked after.

"No, Jorge, please--just give me a few minutes, I'll be
down as quick as I can." She disconnected and turned her
face into her pillow in disgust. *What have I done...how could*

I have been so stupid? Brief flashes of the previous evening came back to her.

How did she end up in her room? Whoever had brought her back here now knew her suite number and had access to it. She must change rooms, immediately. For now, she had to make a supreme effort to look presentable in 15 minutes or less. She threw back the covers and attempted to sit.

Oooooh, she felt like shit. Shivering with the realization she was naked she saw her red dress from the night before neatly draped on the back of an armchair. *How did that get there...don't think about it now. Just try to make it to the bathroom, splash some water on your face.*

She forced herself to stand on the cold tiles and inch her way to the sink. She gulped down the bottled water on the vanity. Foregoing the facewash she opted for the shower and turned it on full blast. Stepping inside she let the hot water rush over her, steadying herself with one hand against the wall.

In the steamy heat she tried to recall the events of the previous night as best she could. She found it appalling that she'd drank so much as to become reckless, incompetent; that wasn't her style at all. Maybe it was more than the drink. Then she remembered Miguel. So different in private from his onstage persona--an irresistible combination of sexy and sweet. She could feel his lips against hers, the pressure of his body pinning her against the wall.

And then nothing.

Did she faint? Had he slipped her something? Forced himself on her? No, impossible. He didn't seem the type. What did Miguel think of her? Had he brought her back here, to tuck into bed his silly groupie? *Groan.* How many times had he done that before?

Grasping the grab bar on the shower wall, Zara hunched over and vomited.

*

The elevator doors opened onto the ground floor and Zara stepped out into the bright morning light. She'd dressed in heavy cotton twill pants and a dri-fit tank top. Steel-toed hikers covered her feet. She'd tied her still-wet hair in a ponytail and dashed on some makeup. Dark sunglasses concealed her red-rimmed eyes. Hardly model perfect, but enough to disguise her misery.

With her Fendi bag slung over her shoulder, she headed to the main entrance where Jorge and another man waited. Based on his white skin and light brown hair, Zara didn't peg the tall guy with Jorge as a local. He stood casually, one hand resting low on his hip and the other holding a cell phone to his ear. He wore a white Henley shirt and jeans that stretched over lean, never-ending legs.

Jorge smiled in relief as he saw her approach. "Ah, Miss Zara, I was beginning to worry. Did you have a late night?"

She felt sheepish, knowing Jorge had no idea what had gone on the night before and comforted by his presence now, taking control of things. "Thank you for caring about me, Jorge. I know mother will be pleased." She put an arm around him, truly glad to see him. When she let go, Jorge introduced her to Dave Parker, one of Flynn's construction supervisors.

Dave extended a hand to Zara. "Pleased to meet you, Miss Flynn. I worked with your father on a few projects, I'm sorry for your loss."

As Zara looked at him, she couldn't remember ever seeing eyes such a nearly cobalt shade of blue. She reached out and gave him her best business handshake, firm and confident. The last thing she wanted was to appear as hung over and out of control as she felt to this new stranger.

Unlike Sr. Verrera's, his hand felt warm and strong. A braided leather bracelet encircled his wrist and she caught a whiff of Lacoste cologne.

"Thank you," she said, breaking contact. The alluring fragrance made her feel even more wretched. She hoped the man...Dave, was it?...wouldn't really look at her at all. She made a conscious effort to look away.

"Shall we?" prompted Jorge, motioning them out to the waiting Mercedes. They moved together out the main entrance doors, Jorge in the lead, Zara in the middle, Dave bringing up the rear.

Jorge opened the back door of the car to let Zara step in, followed by Dave. A utility van bearing the familiar Flynn Enterprises logo idled in the entrance roundabout. It carried a four-man crew of specialty-task team members. The two vehicles pulled in tandem out of the roundabout and down the long drive to the main road.

Heading west on the highway, Zara tried to settle herself enough to rest her head and close her eyes for the duration of the drive. Her thoughts trickled back to Miguel and how exciting the night had been until she passed out. With regret she thought of Bette and Diggy, how they'd tried to stop her from going along with the dark suits. She must remember to call them tonight and apologize for her abominable behaviour and let them know she was all right.

She needed to see about getting another suite, too. *Damn.* There hadn't been time to deal with that this morning. She hadn't left any valuables behind, so a room change could wait until she returned. She should call her mother too, come to think of it. She'd almost nodded off when Dave spoke up.

"So how do you feel about stepping into your father's shoes?"

Zara started at the sound of his voice and turned to face him. "Pardon me?" she asked, not sure if she'd heard him correctly.

"Oh, sorry, I didn't mean to disturb you. Please, go ahead and rest. We've got at least a 40 minute drive."

Zara leaned her head back on the plush leather headrest. "Thank you," she said, running her tongue over her lips. They felt so dry. "My apologies. I did have a rather late night." She reached in her bag for some lip gloss.

As she slicked it on, she felt Dave watching her intently. Her lips shined with the honey-colored gloss on them. After a protracted moment that fell just short of gawking, he looked away out the front windshield.

"Jorge," he said suddenly. "Could you put on some music, please? Not too loud." He turned back to Zara. "Is that alright?" She nodded. Dave relaxed on his side of the rear seat. Soft Latin jazz began to play from the car speakers. They drove on for a bit. Dave sat with his hands folded across his stomach, his head turned away from her, concentrating on the view as the car cruised westward.

"To answer your question," Zara said, "I feel great about it. I'm proud that he considered me worthy of following in his footsteps. I didn't work for him because I didn't want people to think I couldn't make it on my own as an architect. Now it's different, they have to respect me."

Dave turned to her. "That includes me," he said. "You're officially my boss now, as I report to the CEO of the company."

She kept silent for a moment, then let out a light chuckle. "I think I like that idea." She looked straight ahead out the front window. "So where are you from Dave, and how long have you worked for Flynn?"

Dave shifted in his seat, turning his attention to her. "Well, I've been with the EU division for three years now. Before that I started with the company in 2005, in the Boston office. I moved to Boston to attend MIT in 2002, but originally I'm from Thunder Bay." She looked sharply at him. "You know Thunder Bay?" he asked.

"I'm from Montreal, but I was born in Barrie," she said and started to smile.

Dave smiled back. "Small world, eh?"

"Certainly is, eh?" They both laughed, sharing the private joke, neither admitting how the 'eh' phrase was both defining and insulting at the same time. Zara leaned back, enjoying the moment of comic relief. It lessened the throbbing in her head.

"What do you know about El Mirador?" she asked.

"Well, from what I've read, it was a busy holiday resort for the jet-set of the day, in the late 1950s," Dave said. "It went out of business sometime in the 70s. It reverted to the government after that, but never re-developed. Something about a succession plan, the land rights tied up in legal bullshit…sorry, red tape," he corrected, a corner of his mouth quirking up in apology for his slip. "For a long time. Flynn acquired it last year and as far as value, well, you'd have to talk to the local real estate people. Waterfront property must be quite valuable, though. You'd think the government would have forced some action on it, but…things move pretty slow here."

Zara frowned. She'd heard that before. "So, what has Ernesto said? Why did he send you on this trip?"

Dave looked out the window, as if pondering how much he should reveal. After a moment, he inhaled deeply and said, "I'm sure you've noticed the crew traveling with us? The reason El Mirador shut down thirty years ago wasn't lack of business. It burned down and the structure is unstable. That team following us are forensic experts. They'll have priority over investigating the site, not us. We're to keep our distance and do what they say. Understand?"

Zara blinked at him. "Why wouldn't I understand?"

"I didn't say you wouldn't," Dave said, frowning. "Just letting you know, there's something more than just a derelict old building there. Keep a safe distance, wear your safety gear and don't go poking around where you're not supposed to."

Zara looked away, annoyed. Who did this guy think he

was? This was her property, not his, not the companys'. She had more right than anyone to go 'poking around.'

She bit her lip, stewing.

Why would Tristan have put this burden on her shoulders? There didn't seem to be an upside to this deal, other than the location. The structure in ruins, potential trouble in the foundation and millions in projected restoration costs. She almost didn't want to know any more. She had the whole of Flynn Enterprises to worry about, now. Perhaps this project could wait.

The cars slowed as they approached the turnoff to El Mirador. The side road from the east swung to the right and followed an underpass to the seaward side of the highway. Then they hit the gravel path that she and Jorge had taken just days before as they neared the site.

In the morning light, the wreck looked a little different. The exposed steel glinted in the brightness and bits of exterior finishes could be seen on the lee side of the building. Patches of pink and aqua stucco remained, studded with mercury-glass mosaic tiles embedded in spots here and there.

The van parked closest to the building. The four men inside pulled out equipment from the rear and side loading doors. Dave opened the trunk of the Mercedes, which had pulled in behind and to the right of the van to take advantage of what shade it afforded. Inside were hardhats, reflective vests, safety glasses and gloves for each of them. Having read the report thoroughly, Dave also brought SCBA packs in case the air quality was compromised.

He went to confer with the task team as they unloaded specialized monitoring equipment, hand-held scanners and sample containers. Everything fitted into packs that the team could carry on their backs. They moved to the base of the structure and scanned the entrance point. Signalling the all-clear, they waved the others to follow.

Safety gear in place, they crossed the threshold of the main floor. Zara noted the blackened teleposts laid out in a regular grid pattern and the central concrete column of the elevator shaft. Any debris had long been cleaned out by the wind and various scavengers, human and animal alike.

As they approached the dark, open maw of the shaft Chavez, the team leader, directed a high-powered beam into its depths. A flurry of coos and flapping wings surged from the opening, barely missing the heads of the seven people standing near it.

Dave and the task team ducked as the pigeons scattered past them. Zara and Jorge reflexively threw their arms up over their heads to avoid the onslaught. When the air cleared, the team began fitting up portable trouble lights inside the elevator opening and a ladder to descend to the floor below. Pigeon dung stuccoed every visible surface.

One by one they climbed down to the basement level, the dark and dampness palpable as they went. Chavez' handheld gas monitor showed acceptable levels and he gave the okay to remove the air packs. *Thank goodness*, Zara thought, releasing the mask and its accompanying air cylinder from around her face. *Uncomfortable enough in here without those.*

A barrage of odours assaulted them. Sea water and its' fishy smell seeped in through the foundation and left puddles covering most of the ground area. The plop-plop sounds of dripping water echoed all around them and there were underlying scents of sewage and sulphur.

And something else.

Zara couldn't quite put her finger on it. The light-mounts on their hardhats activated in the darkness.

Square concrete columns fanned out in every direction in the same grid pattern as the floor above, charred from the long-ago flames. The team moved towards the far corner, a clear area where columns seemed to be missing. The outer wall on that side had narrow horizontal openings near the top; *For ventilation, no doubt,* Zara thought. As they were above grade, subdued daylight filtered through the openings.

Halting a few meters from the area the team motioned Zara, Jorge and Dave to stop where they were.

The four crewmembers advanced further, setting down their equipment packs and placing sensor stakes into the soft earth around the perimeter. The LED modules at the top of the stakes began to illuminate and cast a sharp greenish light over the scene. The center of the earthen area appeared rough with an almost mushy surface, like oatmeal.

The team spread out, taking readings and samples and sealing them in containers. Zara watched them proceed in methodical fashion, moving from left to right, scanning the area. It measured approximately 10 meters by 20 meters as best she could judge. She saw Dave from the corner of her eye, also watching the men's movements.

The strangely familiar odour was stronger here. She closed her eyes and sniffed, concentrating on it. As the crew moved towards the corner farthest from them, Dave suddenly took a step forward.

"Chavez," he called out. "Hold up...what is that?"

Zara looked towards Chavez, ahead of the other men and about 10 meters away from where she stood. He adjusted his lightmount to see the ground directly around him. He reached down with a gloved hand to pull on an object sticking out from the lumpy earth. All of them drew in a gasping breath.

It looked like a human bone.

CHAPTER EIGHT

"Teléfono, Sr. Bernardo Cruz," announced the concierge. Bernardo looked up from his seat on the plush lobby couch, folded his magazine and tossed it on a coffee table before walking over to the house phone by the front desk. About thirty years old and slight of build, Cruz kept his head shaved, which exposed his protruding ears. He didn't care. The convenience of the close-cropped style made up for it.

He'd been married once, to a local girl his parents had arranged for him, the daughter of family friends. But things did not go well; he discovered his interests were not suited to marriage and left her after only a few years together. His Catholic community openly disapproved. He shook off the memory, reminding himself that he was here, now. He nodded to the concierge and picking up the receiver, spoke softly into it.

"Si?" A smile came over his face as he listened to the comforting voice on the other end. "Si, I will be off work by five. I will be there. Until then, adios." He hung up the receiver, holding back his joy at hearing his lover's voice. It had been a long time and looked forward to resuming that relationship while they were both in the same city.

Bernardo took the elevator down to the parkade. Driving out into the sunlight, he checked the car clock to see how much time he had to get to the office. 12:25 gave him just enough time to arrive by 1:00. Verrera didn't like his staff being late for anything. He checked that his laptop case lay safely stowed behind the passenger seat. He relaxed back into the driver's seat and exhaled, pulling out onto the main road that led to the business district.

He couldn't help but smile at the thought of his date later tonight. His thoughts trailed back to the last time they were together, so exciting, so intense, so...dangerous. But for now, he had better think about finishing his report. He'd stayed at the resort for a few days, following and observing the Flynn girl, as Verrera had requested.

He knew Verrera desperately wanted possession of El Mirador. The project had been expected to continue under general contract with Flynn, or put up for public tender. His boss became angry upon learning the property had been willed to a family member of the Flynn empire.

So far he didn't have much to report, other than a party had left for the site this morning. He recognized Zara of course and assumed the men in the utility van were Flynn employees, but wasn't familiar with the chauffeur nor the other young man who accompanied them. He'd taken plenty of photos though, certain that Verrera would find them interesting.

He pulled into the parking lot of a small centro comerciale. A bay on the far end of the centro housed the field office, where a number of businesses leased warehouse and office space. Hoisting the laptop case over his shoulder by its strap, he locked the car and walked through the glass doors into the dingy office. He moved around the unattended front desk to the hallway leading to two smaller offices and a restroom.

"Ah, Bernardo," Verrera said, as Cruz entered the first office on his left. "Did you have a nice 'vacation,' up at Club Marbella?" he asked with a grin.

"It was very…interesting." Cruz set his laptop on one of two chairs that faced Verrera's desk. "You might even say intriguing."

"Oh," Verrera said, closing the newspaper he'd been reading. "Tell me more. Was the decor appealing?"

"Very much so," Cruz said, thinking of the photos he'd stored on a memory stick. He sat down in the other chair and swiveled the laptop case toward himself. From a side pocket he produced a USB drive and handed it to Verrera. "For your viewing pleasure."

Ignacio cradled the stick between the thumbs and forefingers of both hands. "What other observations have you made? Does the heiress seem at all interested in the investigation?"

Bernardo scratched his right ear, then folded his hands across his lap.

"Senorita Flynn left this morning with a crew from the construction office, along with her driver and another gentleman. They headed west in two vehicles at around 9:40. Before that, Miss Flynn stayed out very, very late last night, attending a stage performance after dinner. She seems to have made the acquaintance of a middle-aged couple from England. They don't appear to have any connection to her or her father's company."

Ignacio tapped the memory stick on the table, thinking. "Esta bien," he said. "Anything else?"

Bernardo continued, "The daytime she spent…indulging herself. The spa, the pool, the beach, et cetera. With the exception of last night, since our meeting on Monday she's laid pretty low. Hard to tell her intentions at this point."

Verrera seemed to consider this. "Well, all we can do is continue to observe. Will you return to the resort tonight?"

"Yes," Bernardo said. *But not for the reasons you think.* He zipped his laptop case closed and stood up. "May I use the other office, I have some paperwork to take care of before heading back."

"Yes, by all means. We'll see you back in the Malaga office on Friday, Si?"

"Si, Friday," Cruz replied, as he crossed the hall.

Verrera rubbed the memory stick between his fingers as if unsure what to do with it. After a long moment, he slipped it into his breast pocket and gathered his things. He left the office without another word.

*

The team stood in front of the open side doors to the van, facing Dave and Zara. As the midday sun glared down on them, Zara removed a glove to wipe her forehead and upper lip. The group stood between the two vehicles, parked a safe distance from the building.

Dave ran his fingers through his tousled forelocks, sweat creating wet tendrils around his forehead and temples. Zara viewed him from the corner of her eye, grateful for her dark glasses. Not only to hide her bloodshot eyes, but so that Dave couldn't tell she was looking.

She took a swig from her water bottle. *He's actually pretty cute.* Clean-shaven, he had a nice straight nose and deep dimple lines set around his highly kissable lips. *Kissable lips? What am I thinking? I have to work with the man.*

She watched a bead of sweat start to trickle down his chest, exposed now that he'd undone the buttons on his shirt. His sleeves were pushed up, revealing well-muscled forearms.

This made her think of Miguel, his bronzed chest glistening in the dimmed lighting of his penthouse. *Oh God, I still have that to deal with.* Would his henchmen be looking for her again? Had they been the ones to undress her and put her to bed last night? The idea made her sizzle with embarrassment. She had to get that room changed right away.

Chavez spoke. "The core samples will tell us more about residual chemicals or trace elements that may have contributed to the structures' degradation. The sensors showed no radioactivity. But as you all saw, the area was clearly quicksand." He gestured to the bone sample they had pulled from the soggy earth, now encased in a sealed plastic exhibit bag. "All this will be taken to a forensic laboratory at the University and we should have some preliminary reports by the end of the week, Monday at the outside. That's it, we'd all better get out of this heat."

The van doors slammed shut and the crew piled in to the passenger seats and made ready to leave. Jorge waited in the Mercedes for Zara and Dave. The two climbed in, grateful for the air conditioning already running inside the car. They slumped into the back seat, feeling wilted from the heat.

Zara reached into her bag and pulled out a facial towel from a small travel pack. Removing her sunglasses, she wiped her face with the soothing cloth.

"Mind if I try one of those?" Dave said.

Zara looked at him in surprise. "Oh, I'm sorry, of course. Here," she said, reaching for the travel pack and offering it to him.

"Wow, those are quite a set of red-eyes you've got there. Allergies?" he asked, pulling a towel from the pack. Zara quickly put her sunglasses on again.

"Uh, no. Just...some new eye makeup I think I reacted to," she said, swallowing the little white lie. Dave put the towel to his face.

"Uh-huh. I must have tried the same brand, then. I think it was called Jack Daniels."

Great, she thought, looking away from him. *A smart-ass. Please God tell me I don't reek of booze.*

Dave grinned. He took her towel that seemed frozen in her hand, added his own and put them both in the trash bin on the floor. "How about a drink when we get back to the resort," he said. "I'll buy."

Chapter Nine

The Ridleys stood at the front desk. "You see, she's not checked out, luv. Just out for the day, sightseeing or shopping or sommat. Didn't she have a work do, this morning?" Diggy said. Bette looked unconvinced.

"So she said…I don't like it, Dig. I felt awful leaving her to go off with them…gents. Scary blokes, gave me the creeps and all, didn't you?" She stamped her plump foot, which bulged out the tops of the bright pink slingback pumps she wore. She spun around to face the desk clerk and asked, "Are you sure she's not left us a message, dear? The Ridleys, room 620?" She wagged a pink gel nail at the girl behind the counter.

"No Senora," she replied in her soft Spanish-accented English. "No messages. Would you like I call housekeeping to see if she leave 'do not disturb'?"

"Can you do that?" Diggy asked.

"Certainly, Senor," she said. "Just one moment, por favor." She went to a side desk and picked up a house phone.

"Thank you…Delores," said Diggy, reading the brass name badge pinned to her uniform vest, nearly bursting its buttons keeping Dolores' ample bust line in check. "Calm down now, sweetie," he said to Bette.

Bette scanned the lobby, as if expecting Zara to pop up from behind a pillar or armchair.

"Senor?" Delores had returned. "Housekeeping say they make up her room already. She not there, but all things are undisturbed."

Diggy sighed.

"Alright, can we leave her a message then, please?" Delores brought out a pen and notepaper, foil-stamped with the Club Marbella logo. He scribbled a few lines, then slid the note back to her. Delores filed it into slot 1004.

"I've asked her to call us the minute she gets in," Diggy said to Bette, putting an arm around her and steering her away from the desk. "Don't worry, luv."

Delores turned back to her computer and began typing. '*Sr. & Sra. Ridley asking questions. Flynn not yet returned. Housekeeping says room undisturbed.*' She poised her index finger over the keyboard. Then she hit send.

*

The blackberry chirped its' text message alert. Zara trudged across the tiled floor of the opulent lobby and ducked toward a couch at the sound of the message coming in. She plopped down on the overstuffed cushions. Pulling out the phone she read, '*Everything OK? Not heard from you in two days, please txt back ASAP.*'

Feeling guilty she'd not contacted her mother sooner, she replied: '*Hi mom yes all OK, very hot here had site visit today, explain more later, call you 2nite.*' Too tired to type anything further, she pressed send.

At one o'clock in the afternoon, Zara already felt exhausted. And hungry. Without any breakfast before her exit this morning, her stomach growled and her head pounded furiously.

She couldn't get out of the Mercedes fast enough. Mr.

Smart-Ass had teased her, then had the nerve to ask her out for cocktails. He didn't quite get the idea that tylenol and a nap ranked higher on her list of priorities at the moment than his riveting company.

She decided to order room service, but first things first. She headed for the front desk.

"Perdoneme," she said, attracting the attention of the desk clerk. Different than the one who'd checked her in. "Hablas Inglés?"

The girl nodded and said yes. Zara smiled, hoping to create enough rapport with her to get what she wanted.

"I need to see about possibly changing rooms, would there be anything else available? I'm in 1004 right now." The desk clerk blinked and frowned.

"We are heavy booked, Senora."

"Are you sure you couldn't move me a little closer to the fourth floor, nearer the spa and gym?" Zara asked. "I'd be happy to take something smaller." She checked the girls' nametag pinned to her chest. 'Marta' it said. "I'm Zara," she added, extending her hand and smiling the best smile she could muster. Marta blushed a little and returned the handshake.

"Marta. Let me check reservations," she said and turned to her computer. She appeared to be running the desk alone. After scrolling through a few screens she said, "There is a standard room on five--not as big as what you have, but with sea view."

"That will be fine, can you send someone to move my things in about an hour?"

"Si, Senora. One hour. I will send the new cardkeys at that time."

Zara tapped the desk counter with the palm of her hand and smiled. "Gracias." She felt instantly better having resolved her security concerns.

She turned to leave when Marta called out, "Por favor, you

have a message, Miss." She plucked the card out of slot 1004 and handed it to Zara.

Shit. She chided herself inwardly for neglecting the Ridleys. "Muchas gracias, " she replied and hurried to the elevators.

*

Dave settled himself in the front seat of the Mercedes after seeing Zara through the entrance doors to Club Marbella.

"Thanks for agreeing to drive us today," he said. "I'm glad Ernie thought to ask you. Sure beats riding in the company bus." He thumbed over at the Flynn vehicle exiting onto the main road heading east.

"De nada," Jorge said with a tip of his chauffeur's cap. "I have worked for Sr. Flynn for many years. It is my privilege to escort Miss Zara wherever she needs to go."

Dave thought about Zara as Jorge spoke her name. She'd been mostly silent on the ride back to the resort, having turned down his offer of a drink. More alcohol was probably the last thing on her mind. She looked hung over, but apparently didn't subscribe to the hair-of-the-dog philosophy.

Having a good view of her from behind as they left the resort that morning, Dave couldn't help remembering how nicely her hips fit into the work pants she wore. Not many women could pull off looking sexy in a pair of Dickies. And the tight-fitting tank top did little to hide her traffic-stopping figure as she'd trooped up and down the site with the rest of the crew. So much for the plump Daddy's girl he'd imagined.

He resolved to ask her out again another time. Her refusal only served to encourage him. That long silky ponytail. The smooth, creamy skin with tawny freckles dotting her nose and cheeks. And those mesmerizing green, albeit bloodshot, eyes. He'd never expected such a delightful new boss.

Whoa big fella, Dave thought, his fantasy screeching to

a halt. *Bad enough getting involved with a co-worker and here you are lusting after the boss.* To top it off, she was Tristan's daughter. A man he respected. And dammit, still felt responsible for.

He jolted himself back to reality. "So how long would that be, your employment with Flynn Enterprises?" Dave asked, realizing what an opportunity he had in talking to someone close to her.

"Oh," Jorge said in a drawn-out voice. "Ever since Marlena recommended me, when Miss Zara was very little."

"You mean Mrs. Flynn hired you?" Dave asked, curious now.

Jorge tipped his head from side to side in an ambiguous response. "Not hired. Recommended. But Sr. Flynn never denied his wife anything, so here I am, twenty years later," he said with a chuckle.

Dave smiled, glad to be getting on with the likeable little man. "You were close friends with Mrs. Flynn?"

Jorge looked at him slyly. "Naturalmente," he said. "We are cousins."

It was Dave's turn to laugh. *Jackpot,* he thought. A treasure trove of information on the lovely Miss Zara Flynn. "Does she plan to stay in Spain, now that she has a role with her father's company?"

Jorge shrugged. "I know Marlena plans to come here, when Miss Zara is ready for her. They are going to Zaragoza for a while and visit family. After that, they planned to return to Montreal. Whether Miss Zara will choose to live here is up to her."

Dave looked out the front window, watching the scenery rush by. "Is that how she got her name, after Zaragoza?" he asked.

"Si, you are muy perceptiva."

Dave laughed. He'd been called a few things before, but

never 'perceptiva.' He glanced sideways at Jorge and saw the man smiling to himself. Did he surmise Dave's interest in his pretty second cousin? If so, he seemed to approve.

CHAPTER TEN

The photo viewer launched on the computer screen. Ignacio closed the door to his home office. His wife and children were not home yet, but he pulled the venetians shut over the windows just in case.

He had to think of a way to dislodge Miss Flynn from the El Mirador project--he'd waited too long and invested too much to lose it now. She seemed a nice, educated girl and he didn't wish to see her harmed or mistreated in any way. Who knows, she might even prove to be a good company executive. But El Mirador was his. It had to be. He sat down in front of the screen and looked at the first photo.

A shot of the Mercedes driven by Flynn's man, Jorge Allesandro. Next. Distance shot of Allesandro and Flynn standing 50 metres away from the site. Next. Zara Flynn walking into the Club Marbella entrance. Next. Flynn swiping the cardkey of room 1004. Next. Flynn at lunch in Cafe Marbella. Next. Flynn now seated at another table with two unlikely looking characters. An overweight woman in a garish outfit and a thin gentleman with combed-back grey hair.

Hmm, these must be the English couple Cruz mentioned. Were they friends, relatives? He zoomed in with the mouse, but didn't recognize either of them. He pulled up the print menu and sent the image to a photo printer on an adjoining desk, then clicked Next.

Uninteresting photo of Club lobby. Next. Photo of stage entrance, the marquee above it reading 'appearing this week only, exclusive...' Next. View of suite balcony...presumably 1004? Looked like a long drop to the ground from there. Verrera's twisted mind formed potential scenarios by which to solve his little problem.

The next several photos were of the hotel layout and he skimmed through them not seeing anything of note. He looked over at the printer tray which now held three or four sheets. He got up from his computer desk to retrieve them. He couldn't afford to leave anything lying around.

He enjoyed his home office. Surveying the room, he complimented himself on the decor. The dark wine-colored walls, white trim and ample bookcases. A humidor which carefully stewarded his collection of exotic cigars hid behind a foldout bar cabinet. His one weakness. He picked up the prints and returned to his desk.

Scrolling through more pictures, he saw the same elderly couple with Flynn in the dining room. Eating, laughing and drinking. He zoomed in on the cocktail in Flynn's hand, for reference. Margarita appeared to be a favourite. He filed this away in a corner of his brain. Next.

Ignacio froze. There, in full view of the frame was Flynn, reclining in a deck chair, her hair flayed out across the towel on which she lay. The photo appeared taken from above, giving the image a voyeuristic edge. Save for her bikini bottoms, she was naked.

He stared in disbelief at the almond-white skin, glossy lips and most noticeably, the round, exquisite breasts in the centre of the frame.

"Dios mío," he swore in a whisper. He wrestled with

his emotions, knowing he should click to the next image immediately. But the mouse pointer stayed poised over the print command. In a weak instant, he clicked it.

No sooner had he released the mouse button when he heard the latch on the oak front door give a click, followed by the swishing sound of its' opening. He'd left his car on the drivepad, so they all knew he was home. His family came bumping and crunching into the front room just outside his office, shopping bags rattling and shoes clunking.

"Padre! Padre!" he heard his daughter Daniela squealing as she rushed for his office door. He quickly shut off the computer's monitor and snatched the USB stick from its slot. The door burst open.

"Tu est aqui!" Daniela exclaimed. She bounded into the room with her usual excitement whenever daddy came home early. He often worked late or went away on business. She jumped into his arms, nearly knocking the USB stick from his hand. In a moment his youngest daughter Ericka joined them, clapping her hands, anxious for her turn on daddy's lap.

"Niñas, niñas," he said, "one at a time. Come, let's go to the kitchen and help your mother." He lowered Daniela to the floor and slipped the stick into his pants pocket. He took Ericka by the hand and led them both out of the room, closing the office door. He'd come back to tidy up, he assured himself. In the kitchen, his wife Carmella carried shopping bags in from the car. The girls rushed past her into the back garden to play.

"Hola, my dear," Ignacio said, reaching to take the bags from her. A short, portly woman, Carmella brushed a strand of curly dark hair off her forehead, looking flushed from the heat outdoors and from carrying the heavy bags.

"There's more in the car," she said in a monotone, breathing heavily from exertion. She set her purse down on a kitchen stool and began to unpack the first bag.

"I'll get them," Ignacio said, recognizing all too well the annoyance in her voice. Unlike his daughters, Carmella did not appreciate him coming home early. It seemed to upset her routine, so he was eager to do whatever she asked to avoid an argument.

He retrieved three more bags of groceries from the rear seat of her little car, an economic Punta sedan he'd picked out for her several years ago. Carrying them back into the kitchen, he set them down on the opposite counter where Carmella stood pulling out cans and packages to be stored in the pantry. Ignacio did the same with his bags.

"What are you doing home at this time of day," she asked, with her back turned to him. He thought for a moment how he should answer to elicit the least hostile response.

"Oh, well, we were working in the field office today, at the Centro. We finished early, but it became too late to drive all the way back to Malaga. So here I am." He paused. "The girls seem pleased." Carmella didn't say anything but continued to put her groceries away. Silence prevailed for a few minutes as the two of them worked in the kitchen without speaking.

"I think you should work more." Carmella said. "I can handle things here; you're just in the way when you come home early." Ignacio sighed. He worried about her, being overweight and with high blood pressure. And being irritated all the time, as she seemed to be lately, wasn't helping her health.

Like Bernardo, his family had 'arranged' his match for him. Carmella's father was well off, so the pairing should have been prosperous. However, apparently not so prosperous as she'd hoped, always hinting at getting a bigger house, better cars, better clothes and toys for her and her daughters.

She'd nearly died when Ericka was born. The pregnancy and delivery took a toll on her precarious health. His father in law being sick and elderly now, it was unclear how much estate might be left to Carmella when he did pass on.

He shrugged and replied, "I don't do it very often, cariña. I'm not being in the way, I am trying to help you. You might have fainted carrying in all those bags. You should work less and let me do more," he suggested. This statement he felt smug with, having thought of it so quickly and coming off more brilliant than he'd intended.

Carmella set a can of tomatoes down on the counter, ever so firmly, making a statement without actually slamming it and turned to face him.

"I said, I can handle things, I don't need you underfoot. I need you out there, earning more money." Ignacio looked down at his hands, which he placed flat on the counter and breathed in and out so he could speak calmly.

"I am at the top of my wage scale with the county. Until next years budget, I won't see a raise, you know that. I am working on some things; I've only just started getting my own contracting business off the ground. It takes time, I have to be patient."

She tapped her pudgy fingers on the marble countertop.

"*You* have to be patient, but I don't. I shouldn't have to be. My father can provide for me just as well or better than you."

Ignacio ran his hand over his bald head, knowing his efforts to avoid a quarrel were in vain. "Cami, your father is not well. I can provide for you and the girls. I always have and I always will. And it will be even better when I close some deals with my business. I don't want you to worry about this anymore and I don't want to argue. It's bad for you."

She sniffed and turned back to her groceries. Ignacio put away the last of the items from his bags and went to find his girls. He hoped they'd not overheard their conversation.

He went to the garden, but they'd either gone back inside or to the park down the street. *They would have told us if they'd done that*, he thought. They were raised to always let mama and papa know where they were and to ask permission.

He went around to the front of the house, but didn't see them there either.

He noticed some trampled flowers near the front steps. He bent down to straighten them and pick off the crushed blossoms. A scream echoed from inside. He bolted through the front door, vaulting towards the sound of his daughters who'd found their way back to the kitchen.

Carmella lay on the floor on her side, her eyes rolled upwards and hands pressed to her chest. Ignacio called out in anguish and Daniela knelt beside her while Ericka stood with her back against the kitchen cabinets, terrified. "Madre, Madre," they screamed. He picked up the phone and dialed the police, fighting back tears.

Chapter Eleven

Sitting in an armchair in her new room, Zara hung up the phone. She felt better now, having assured the Ridleys of her welfare and apologizing for not calling them earlier. Under the circumstances, they understood she had a job to do and forgave her for rushing out of the hotel without contacting them that morning.

She also let them know her new room location, so they could call her any time or stop by. Bette sounded pleased at this news. She seemed to have taken a maternal interest in Zara that grew stronger by the minute.

She set her empty glass of Perrier on the room service tray next to the remains of her lunch. Having something to eat killed her hangover but made her sleepy. A nap wouldn't be out of line. Lying on the bed, she pulled her cell phone out of her bag and dialed her mother. It would be very early in the morning in Ontario.

"Hola," came her mother's pleasant voice, in spite of the early hour.

"Hi, Mom."

"Oh, darling, it's you, gracias a Dios. Como esta?"

"Fine, Mom. Sorry for not calling before--you got my texts?"

"Si, querida, I'm so glad to hear from you. How are things going, are you getting much done? What you wanted to?"

Zara sighed. "I'm working on it, Mom. And I'm going to Dad's office tomorrow to get familiar with everything. We went to the site this morning. You won't believe what we found." Marlena waited for her to continue. "It's a wreck. The structure is decades old, looks like a bomb hit it and, get this. It's sitting over a field of quicksand. I don't understand why that could be. They'd know where quicksand was before starting construction. Did Dad ever talk about El Mirador, or explain why he bought it?"

Marlena hesitated before answering. "Not really. But you know your father, always 'the big picture.' He never did anything without purpose, even if it wasn't obvious to others. I knew you would inherit the business and with it a number of different properties, but remember, as a private sale El Mirador is yours outright. You can do with it whatever you wish. Dad had a reason and I'm sure you'll figure it out. You're a brilliant young woman. I should know, I raised you."

Zara laughed. "Can't argue with that, Mom. I'll keep you posted. Jorge says hi. He went to see Elena the other day."

"Muy bien," Marlena said. "I hope he'll come with us to Zaragoza. He needs to see his mother. Marcela hasn't been well."

Zara hadn't thought about Great-Aunt Marcela for a long time. While true she was Jorge's mother the family did not speak of it, Marcela being unmarried at the time of his birth. A bit of a recluse, she didn't attend family functions. All she remembered about Marcela were the burn scars on her face and arms and how they'd frightened her as a child.

"Have you booked your flight yet, Mom? Because I'm not

sure how soon we'll be able to do that, get away to Zaragoza, I mean."

"I'll wait to hear from you. Dad has open tickets with the airlines, remember? No hay problema."

Right, Zara thought. *No problema.* "Okay Mom. We'll talk to you soon, bye."

"Adios, querida."

Zara disconnected. 'Dear one,' her mother called her. She thought of when she was a little girl, playing in the sandbox, going to the park, riding a bicycle. Before long she drifted off to sleep, the cell phone still cradled in her hand.

*

At six o'clock, Delores logged off her computer, tidied up her papers and put fresh mints in the silver tray next to the floral arrangement at the end of the reception desk. She called into the back room, "Adios, Marta, I'm leaving for the day." A mumbled "Okay" issued from inside.

Finished her day shift, Delores picked up her handbag from under the counter and headed down the hallway to the staff lounge. A few people lingered there, watching soccer on the lone TV in the room. Two of the housekeepers giggled over a trashy magazine. Each said hello as she passed by.

Delores opened her locker and took out a duffel bag and sweater. She checked her makeup in the room's only mirror. Pursing her lips, she pulled a tube of lipstick from her handbag and slicked some extra color on. Then she checked the duffel bag to make sure she had everything she needed for the evening ahead. Perfume, shoes, sexy outfit; all in place.

She zipped the bag closed, grabbed her purse and sweater and left the room. She walked past the housekeepers again on her way out, hiding a smirk as she entered the corridor, looking both ways to make sure no one saw her before pushing the button for the service elevator at the end of the hall.

*

Seeing as his boss had left early, Bernardo shut down his laptop in the scrungy cubicle across from where Verrera had been working. No reason not to get a head start on his evening. He'd tried hard to put it out of his mind for the afternoon, focusing on his work to pass the time. But no use. He felt he would scream if he sat still much longer. The temptation of what awaited him back at the Club made him itch in places that couldn't be scratched in public.

He looked forward to leaving the spare, stuffy workspace of the field office. The main office in Malaga was much nicer, much more appropriate for a savvy young executive on the rise such as himself. He planned to be a great deal more than Verrera's assistant. Only a stepping-stone to better things, he'd performed some distasteful duties already in the six months he had been at this job. Soon it would be time to move on.

He slipped on his blazer that hung on the back of the well-worn office chair while looking at the pale, undecorated walls. *Yes,* he thought, *I will be moving on very soon*. He locked the metal and glass entrance door as he went out. He got into his car, started the engine and the air conditioning. Feeling uplifted, he peeled recklessly out of the parking lot, screeching his tires and leaving tracks as he started back to Club Marbella.

The sea looked lovely in the late afternoon sun. Bernardo turned off the air conditioning, opting for the top down on his little convertible. Salsa music boomed from the stereo and he tapped his fingers in time on the steering wheel, thoroughly enjoying the triple sensations of wind against his face, sun on his shoulders and pavement disappearing beneath his wheels.

He felt free and light, as bubbly as the breakers striking the beach below. He slowed as he approached the gates of the Club, but sped up on the long driveway to the hotel, just for effect. He entered the underground parkade and cruised to his parking stall, braking abruptly to squeal the tires.

His studio room on the eighth floor boasted a terrific view, but it held no interest for him tonight. He showered and changed clothes, then went about arranging everything just so. A vase of red roses on the nightstand, chilled bottle of champagne from the mini-fridge set out on a console table with two glasses. He shut all the blinds and draperies, dimmed all the lights and left the room. He slipped one of his cardkeys in the green urn by the elevators and went down to the cocktail lounge to wait.

*

The third floor didn't have any guest suites. Mostly utility and storage rooms, a few salons and a larger open space for hospitality receptions. Delores stepped off the service elevator and went down a back corridor that circled the central hospitality room, arriving at an inconspicuous door on the far left. She pulled out the magnetic badge that hung on a lanyard around her neck and swiped it in the cardlock. The room stored linens, pillows and draperies piled in neat stacks on aisles of shelving.

At the end of the centre aisles, a few shelving units had been removed creating a hidden rectangular space between the shelf towers and the back wall of the room. Draperies hung around it like Persian rugs in a marketplace.

Parting the curtains, Delores stepped inside the little makeshift room where a low divan overflowing with satin-covered pillows of all shapes and sizes had been placed. The striped damask upholstery of the curve-backed divan further enhanced the middle-eastern look. Delores set down her bag, withdrew an outfit and began to change.

With the costume in place, she arranged herself provocatively on the divan, pleased with how the gauzy veils and skimpy, spangled two-piece suit looked on her. She'd also brought a burner and some incense sticks, which she lit and set on the floor. Inhaling the heady smoke, she relaxed and waited for her guest to arrive.

*

Bernardo rubbed his palms together trying to dispel the familiar sweaty fear that took over him on occasions such as this. The ride up the elevator seemed interminable. He'd downed a few scotch in the lounge, just enough to feel primed for his rendezvous. His guest liked to arrive unobserved.

He approached the door to his room, took out his second cardkey and entered. The lights were out except for the glow from the strip lighting around the perimeter of the room. A figure stood near the window and he went toward it. Reaching out, he touched her on the shoulder and she turned to him, the face in shadows. Bernardo knew exactly who it was. "Michelle," he whispered softly.

"Si," the husky voice replied. Blonde tonight, she'd changed her hair since last time. A white gown with a deep split in the skirt reached up to the top of the thigh, revealing a leg sheathed in gartered stockings that shimmered in the dim light.

He touched her leg, ran his hand up her thigh and pulled her upper body close with his other arm. He felt drunk just smelling the dark and spicy cologne, his lips searching in the dark.

They kissed, slowly at first. They moved towards the bed, where he turned her to face away from him. Bernardo unzipped the lovely gown, slipped the shoulder straps off and let it fall to the floor. Then he pushed her roughly onto the bed on her stomach and began to undo his pants.

His gaze fixated on the shapely buttocks in front of him as he ripped the condom from its package. The black garter straps that stretched diagonally across them and held the shiny stockings in place heightened his desire. Fully aroused, he ran his hands across her taut cheeks and placed himself between them. He held on to her somewhat bony hips as he made love to her in his favourite position, pumping angrily and imagining the low grunting sounds he heard as feminine sighs of ecstasy.

*

"What do you mean, he's not coming?" demanded Delores. Her cell phone had rung after waiting about an hour in her drapery-walled enclave. He'd been late before. Not unusual, having to dodge photographers and reporters wherever he traveled. But never had she received calls from his bodyguards, expressing his regrets that he must reschedule their 'appointment.'

"Well, tell him he can go straight to el Diablo," she snapped and hung up. "Madre de dios," she muttered and punched one of the silky pillows on the divan. She threw another one across the little room where it struck one of the drapes and knocked it down. More than angry, she now felt silly dressed in this get-up, waiting for no one.

Where the hell was he? After all she'd done for him. Did he think she appreciated being called so late last night, just to come back to work and tuck little miss red dress into bed? Silly cow, who couldn't hold her liquor.

Delores had managed to usher her back to the tenth floor unnoticed, deposited her into her room and undressed her. She'd even thought about stealing the pretty red dress, but reasoned that it couldn't possibly have fit her.

From now on, she thought, *he'll be the one to dress up and wait for me!*

CHAPTER TWELVE

Miguel waved to Zara from the boat. He wore his all-white suit that she'd seen him in on stage, his hair blowing in the breeze off the Mediterranean. She waved back to him as best she could, keeping one hand on the tow handle, skiing bravely behind the churning wake of the speedboat.

It was her first time on water skis. Miguel had taught her in just one afternoon, being an expert and having won many competitions. Suddenly she hit the cross-wake of another craft that passed by and tumbled into the water. She tasted the salt on her lips, heard no sound as her head slipped beneath the surface.

In an instant, she felt Miguel's arms around her. He'd cut the motor and dived off the stern of the boat to get to her, ensuring her safety. They bobbed up and down in the crystal blue sea, splashing each other playfully and laughing while he held her close. He kissed her and licked his lips, making a show of how good and salty she tasted. She splashed him again and they swam back to the boat together.

The next thing she knew, they lay naked on the swim deck of the boat, she on her back looking up at his face framed by the incredible blue of the sky. Under the hot sun, his hands stroked her nude body and she giggled, embarrassed that the driver might see them. Of course, he was paid *not* to see them. Why should she worry, or care?

His lips were about to touch hers, his face so close she could feel the heat from it when a booming claxon sounded, like the signal of a cruise ship leaving port. Startled, Miguel covered her body with his, bending his head down against the curve of her neck.

Then she could see the boat driver clearly, looking straight at them. She felt guilty, brazenly lying here in the open air with this crazy man. Especially when the driver looked exactly like...Dave.

Zara woke with a rushing sound in her ears, like an ocean wave that receded as she gained consciousness. Breathing heavily, her heart pounding, it took a moment to recall her surroundings. The room became lighter as she opened her eyes and realized she'd been dreaming.

She expelled a long breath of air as if she'd just run a marathon. In those first few seconds, the dream seemed incredibly clear. The exciting touch of Miguel the Latin superstar followed by the stern reality of Dave Parker the construction boss.

Oddly, she'd felt guilt in the dream sequence, having the distinct impression she somehow belonged to Dave and shouldn't have been messing with Miguel or anybody else. In the next instant, the whole scene faded and she couldn't remember what she'd been dreaming about at all, like most dreams. She rolled over and checked the bedside clock. 5:05. Was that a.m. or p.m.?

Pale light emanated from the windows. *Must be morning. I've slept for over 12 hours.* She closed her eyes again for a few minutes before forcing herself out of bed and into the shower.

Knowing better than to skip breakfast this time, Zara went

down to the café and sat at a little table to enjoy a plate of sliced fruit and a croissant. She'd filled a travel mug with coffee from the buffet and waved when Bette and Diggy entered the café.

Bette bustled over, wearing a bright green and purple print dress with matching green slingbacks. Diggy followed her in his ever-casual style, brown slacks and a short-sleeved cotton shirt. He'd actually gone a bit wild today. The shirt had a Hawaiian pattern on it.

They joined her at the next table, pulling their chairs close so Bette could interrogate her on her whereabouts Tuesday night.

"So, what happened then," she asked in concerned excitement. "So glad you're safe, luv. Worried sick, weren't we Dig? Who were them gents?" Bette even wore matching green-rimmed sunglasses, completing the English tourist look.

Plenty of English people roamed the Costa del Sol. Only a short flight from Heathrow it made a popular destination for Brit vacationers. You could tell by the fish and chip shops in every little town on the highway. Zara sipped her coffee, knowing she would have to come clean with Bette sooner or later. No time like the present.

"They work for someone in this hotel," she said. "Someone very famous, who apparently felt inclined to invite me to a party."

"Give over!" said Bette in a low voice. "Not…not Mickey, surely. You're joking!" Zara took another sip from the travel mug.

"Let's just leave it at, someone, male…and musical…and performing in this hotel. And no, I did not get taken advantage of."

Bette's mouth dropped open. "Why the hell not, if it was flaming Mickey Mountain taking the advantage!"

Bette," Diggy cautioned. "Mind yourself, now."

Bette elbowed him.

"I'm just having a little fun and all. What was he like, then, eh?"

Zara shook her head. "Nothing happened. We had some champagne and I...blacked out. The next thing I knew, I woke up in my room."

Bette looked genuinely alarmed.

"Well who put you there then, if you passed out?"

Zara shrugged. "I must have walked. I'm fine--nothing happened, really." She left out the waking up naked part, which still made her burn when she thought about who might have undressed her.

Jorge waved to her from the cafe doors. Zara pushed her plate away, picked up her mug and bag and stood to leave. "I've got to go, folks. My ride is here and I'm going to work today," she said, feeling quite proud. She had a purpose here after all, despite the shenanigans of the first few days.

Diggy stood. "Glad to see you're alright lass; call us anytime if you need sommat. Go build something pretty, eh?"

Zara saluted and said "Roight, mate!" in a mock English accent.

Bette chimed in. "Let's plan a trip out to Gib on the weekend. Got some lovely pubs and shops there, we'll arrange it while you're at work, eh?"

"Sounds fine," Zara said as she hurried to make an exit from the café and her overprotective guardians.

The route into Malaga's city centre veered away from the sea and soon, tall buildings blocked the view. Jorge parked the Mercedes in front of a modern office building a few blocks off the main thoroughfare. Though not owned by Flynn Enterprises, the company leased an entire floor in it, where Ernesto and others ran the Andalusian operations. Her father also kept an office here in which she could work; at least for today.

In the back of her mind, she knew she really hadn't come to grips with her father's death. Too many unanswered questions left her unable to achieve closure. These people at Flynn probably knew more about him and the circumstances of his death than she did.

They took the elevator to the eighth floor and saw the steel double doors bearing the Flynn logo cast in metal. Centred over the two doors, it split cleverly in half when opened. Zara thought the hard-edged industrial look quite impressive, despite being only a regional office. London housed the HQ, but offices similar to this one existed in Hong Kong, Sydney, Montreal and Boston. Jorge pulled on the long vertical handles of the door, crafted from solid bar stock and polished to a fine sheen. The doors parted and Zara entered the room.

A half-dozen people surrounded the reception desk. All of them turned as she walked in, including Ernesto. He started everyone in the room applauding. They were all smiling, apparently anticipating her arrival. Ernesto came over and took her hand. "Buenas días, Miss Flynn. I've been telling everyone about you and they're anxious to meet Tristan's daughter. We're a close-knit group here. A testament to him."

He began to introduce her. Armand, the accountant; Pilar, the round-faced receptionist with dark hair cut in a chin-length bob. Two draftsmen, Chico and Efren sat next to each other at their CADD stations. A few younger women, file clerks and a proposal writer also nodded in greeting. Dave stood in the doorway of an adjoining coffee room. His dimples creased as he smiled at her. He folded his arms and leaned against the doorframe.

"Hi," he said simply, no further words necessary. An unspoken bond had already begun forming between them. She tilted her head a bit, as if seeing him in a new light.

"Hi." A good deal more than 'cute,' she liked his longish, sandy brown hair that curled up at the ends, making him look more like a surf bum than an engineer. And the neatly trimmed sideburns he'd given himself--she hadn't noticed those the other day. But she did remember those eyes, all of a sudden.

Cobalt blue, staring disapprovingly at her in a dream.

The image fragment flashed in her brain, unsettling her. She broke her gaze away from him.

He spoke to Ernesto. "Well, let's give the lady a tour, shall we. I'm sure she'd like to see her office."

Ernesto nodded, placing his hands together with palms facing.

"By all means. Zara? This way," he gestured to his left down a short hallway. Zara followed Ernesto to the room at the end, with Dave falling in behind her. She sensed him only a few feet away and found herself wondering if she'd dressed appropriately.

Her hair hung in a single braid down her back. She'd chosen a navy blue skirt, the kind with the flippy edges at the hem that swirled back and forth as she walked and a short-sleeved v-neck sweater. Did the neckline reveal too much cleavage? Her favourite silver necklace with the dolphin pendant dangled just above it. A smashing pair of navy pumps showed off her legs.

Dave nearly bumped into her as she stopped short inside the doorway of Tristan's well-appointed office. She floated to the center of the room, turning a slow 360 to view the walls, adorned with a strategic mix of paintings, awards and architectural drawings. A huge mahogany desk commanded the space, paired with a large leather swivel chair. A large flat screen monitor rested on the desktop.

Under a window at one end of the room sat a familiar-looking drafting table. On either side of it stood matching mahogany bookcases filled with volumes of reference books, technical manuals and architectural publications. She longed to sit at that table, as if the vellum sheets laid out on it called to her along with the large carousel of pencils and tools next to it. She walked over, reached out and touched all the items. Dave and Ernesto exchanged glances.

"Can I get you a coffee, ma'am?" Dave said, to break the silence. He said it in a deferential tone, but tongue-in-cheek, underlining the fact she was now his boss. She laughed, and spun around to face the two of them, a big smile on her face.

"Yes, please."

The three of them spent the morning reviewing project plans, each at various stages of completion. A nearly finished high-rise in Estepona. An apartment building here in Malaga, as well as a shopping complex. Renovations for two resorts on the Mijas-Costa and most interesting of all, an upgrade to the stadium of the Plaza de Toros at Ronda.

And El Mirador.

"The forensics reports are not yet in," Ernesto confided. He, Dave and Zara sat at the long table in the center of his office surrounded by drawings and photos. Dave had taken a chair next to her and she felt his arm touching hers as they propped their elbows on the table. She tried to ignore it, but the heat spot it created kept drawing her attention, as did the return appearance of Rene Lacoste. *Damn, he smelled good.* "What were your impressions of the site?" Ernesto asked.

Dave spoke first. "We stayed out of the way as much as possible, as you asked. But when we found the bones, we got a little closer. I'm not an anatomy expert, so I couldn't tell you if they were animal or human. The fact they were near the surface suggests the victim was recent, or the bones were placed there from somewhere else."

"And did you find evidence of explosives?"

Dave sent him a dark glance. He shook his head. "The team scanned for residual chemicals as well as live sets, mines; if a bomb went off there, it was a long time ago." Ernesto looked at Zara overtop of his eyeglasses.

"What were your feelings, Zara?" She sat in a swivel chair

with her arms folded, taking in all the information. *Explosives?* Her lower lip protruded in thought.

"It felt…contrived." The two men's eyebrows raised at the word.

"How so?" Ernesto asked.

"The quicksand, it didn't fit. Who would build over top of it? And why? It's as if the quicksand was *put* there, although I don't know how you'd do that, to disguise something."

"Or to draw attention to it," Dave said. "Make people watch this hand," he raised his left hand in the air, "when they should be watching this hand." He lowered his right hand below the table.

"Quicksand does occur naturally in a coastal environment," Ernesto said. "Particularly at low tide. Underground water, salt water, separates the sand granules from each other making the surface unstable."

"Could it have developed after the original completion of the building? The water level might have been different 30 or 40 years ago," Dave said.

Ernesto considered this. "Tal vez, maybe. But it would still be possible to build around the area. The depth of quicksand wouldn't be great."

Zara leaned forward. "As I said, the question is why? There are miles of beach there. Why that spot?"

"A very good question, Zara. Now that you're in charge, how would you like to proceed?" Ernesto asked.

"Well, I thought I'd be in the resort business when I found out the property belonged to me. Can we find more information on what the place was like in its' heyday? It looks so lonely and abandoned. It's fascinating to think about what went on there. I'd like to see it restored."

She sighed, knowing how unrealistic that sounded.

"But if you feel it's better just tearing it down for public safety reasons, I'm okay with that." She held up one of the project photos. "We can always build another hotel, right?"

"Some research would be prudent, in any case," Ernesto said.

He looked at Dave, who looked back at him, then to Zara, and back to Ernesto.

"You want me to do the research?" Dave asked, sounding surprised.

Ernesto nodded. "You have access to all the online archives. Try the tourism office, too. Zara, would you like to get started on some drawing projects in the meantime?"

"I'd love to. For El Mirador?"

"Let's wait to see what we can find out," Ernesto said. "I think Chico is running into some issues with the Estepona high-rise. Why don't you meet with him and see what you can do on that one to start with."

Zara nodded, but added, "I think Dave has more important things to do than fact-find. How about we do some internet searches first, let our fingers do the walking?" She looked over at Dave, who didn't seem too thrilled with his assignment. In truth, she wanted a little space from him. He was a distraction. She really needed to focus on some work right now.

"Honestly Ern, I really should be checking in with my crews. Pilar can help with the web search," Dave said. Ernesto turned back to the papers in a file folder in front of him and sighed.

"I thought I'd do the research myself," Zara said. "That computer does work, doesn't it?" She thumbed in the direction of Tristan's office next door to Ernesto's.

"Of course, wireless, too." Ernesto said.

She gripped the armrests on her chair and stood up, matter-of-factly. "I can have a word with Chico, get my feet wet in that, and get the background on El Mirador at the same time. You needn't bother Dave, I'm sure he's tired of babysitting me."

Dave stood as well. "You're the boss," he said, sounding

relieved. "Ernie, I'll call in later and let you know if I'll be in tomorrow. I might have to go out to Gib and see suppliers."

"Well," Ernesto said, closing his file folder. "Looks like the two of you don't need any motivational speeches. Seguir, carry on." They both turned to leave. As Dave held the door for Zara, she asked,

"What's 'Gib'? Some friends of mine wanted to take a trip there."

"Oh, I meant Gibraltar, have you not been there?" he asked.

"I think you know where I've been, Dave. I only got here four days ago and so far I've spent two of them with you," she said flatly.

"You mean it's your first time to Spain? I thought your dad would have brought you here on vacation. Gibraltar, you know, the Rock?"

Of course she'd been to Spain before. She'd never heard Gibraltar referred to as 'Gib' until today and felt a little foolish as the realization dawned on her. "Oh, right. To be honest, I never did stop there," she said, formulating a defence. "I... actually slept in the car as we passed through this time." *Lame, but true.*

One corner of his mouth curved up in a half-smile. "That's a shame. One of the great wonders of the world, you know." The facetious grin blossomed the rest of the way across his lips. "Anyway, it's British territory and a major shipping port. So it's easy to get building supplies, electronics, booze, anything. And really good fish and chips. Maybe you'd like to come along. Plenty of boutiques there, too."

She shot him a patronizing look as she felt a mild burn rising in her cheeks. He appeared to take great pleasure in making fun of her. He backpedalled, saying, "But you could always hang with me at the lumberyard if shopping's not your thing. That's always exciting."

Zara considered it, leaving a purposeful silence hanging

in the air. "I really should get to work. I wouldn't want these good people to think I'm the Princess CEO."

Unaffected by the awkward pause, Dave cocked his head to one side, conceding her point. "I suppose not. Well, I'll be heading out first thing and I'd have to go right past your hotel anyway." He reached into his shirt pocket for a business card and handed it to her. "My cell number's on the card; give me a call around 8 a.m. if you change your mind."

She took the card and read it. It had the Flynn banner at the top, his name in the middle and contact info at the bottom. 'David J. Parker, CET, B.Sc., Project Supervisor.' She noted 'smart-ass' was not part of his title. "I'll think about it. Thanks."

Dave smiled again, turned and went down the hall to his own office past the coffee room. Walking away from her, she thought of a new definition of smart ass and made a mental note of which door was his. It might be interesting to see how he kept his work area--neat freak or pack rat?

Flapping the card thoughtfully against her palm, she watched him and his cute butt disappear into his office, then turned and went back into hers. *My office,* she thought. She'd have to get used to that idea. She could never replace her father, but she would damned well give it her best shot.

She sat at the drafting table and had a good look at the drawings still taped to it. Elevation views of a new project. The title block read 'Los Tiedes.' A circular kind of building with three storeys and a cone-shaped roof. A sort of modern take on a lighthouse, with narrow slotted windows on the sides and big glass ones all around the top floor.

Several rolled blueprints were stored upright in a nearby taboret table. She pulled one out and spread it on the desk--the shopping complex here in Malaga. She pulled out another. A high-rise project and another, a townhouse development. She replaced them in the slots they came from. A few loose sheets lay on one corner of the table. These seemed more like sketches, perspective renderings intended for proposal purposes.

To her surprise, they appeared to be residential plans. Large private villas that looked like homes for the very rich. Strange. Her father didn't ordinarily do private residences. The titles written in stylized architectural lettering at the bottom right of each drawing caught her attention. 'La Marlena' read one. Her mother's name. 'La Dulce Zara' read another. Were these her father's pet projects, designing homes for private clients? Or perhaps the very people he'd named them after?

Beautiful, but no indication that the designs were actually under construction. Just ideas on paper. Great ideas, because they were all 'green' designs, too. Eco-friendly. That was her Dad's work, for sure. She decided they would look great framed and on the walls of the office. She looked around for a portfolio cover and slipped the drawings inside, placing it in the top drawer of the desk.

Now she could have a chat with Chico and begin some real work.

CHAPTER THIRTEEN

Bernardo listened to his voicemail with alarm. Verrera left a choked message that his wife was in hospital recovering from a heart attack and that he wouldn't be at the office until further notice. He'd taken his daughters to a relative's house out of town, and had spent night and day at the hospital.

He asked Bernardo to go to the Malaga office in his place. He pressed 'save' to store the message and returned his cell phone to his pocket. Too bad. He was having such a nice morning remembering last night's exciting events. He chose to have lunch at a favorite bistro across the avenue from the Club.

From the Malaga office, he wouldn't be able to monitor Flynn's private life for the next little while. But there were more important matters to attend to. He sipped the last of his coffee, then reached for his cell phone again and scrolled through his contacts to find 'Michelle.' His pulse quickened just seeing the name in writing and tried to suppress his anticipation of their next meeting. He began to text… *'gracias for last night, miss u already, can't wait til Friday.'* Send.

Next, he called the office and left a message saying he

would be there in the morning to cover for Verrera. That way, he'd have time to pay a visit to El Mirador this afternoon. He placed his napkin over his plate, picked up his laptop case and headed for his car.

*

Delores worked her afternoon shift, her anger still smoldering at being stood up the previous night. She supposed she should have expected it; she wasn't exactly the only doll in the toy box, after all. She'd been responsible for most of the 'play dates'.

How many meetings had she arranged for him? Twenty? Thirty? Always a different girl, always exactly as requested. Perhaps they'd get in touch with her today, to explain and apologize and arrange an alternate meeting to make it up to her.

This made her feel a bit better and decided to hold on to this thought for now. She sighed. Despite her anger, being in the company of the fabulous Miguel Montana was not a privilege to take for granted. She knew she would make herself available whenever he asked.

She appraised herself in the staff lounge mirror. What was not to like? Brunette hair, flashing eyes. Large breasts firmly displayed in a pushup bra, creating noticeable cleavage even in the plain-collared shirt and vest of the Club uniform. She undid just one more button, hoping the manager on shift wouldn't give her trouble about it and marched out to the front desk.

She greeted her co-worker, Linda, who had come on the morning shift to relieve Marta.

"Buenas tardes, Delores," Linda replied. "I'd button up that shirt if I were you. Garcia is on today." Delores ignored her and logged in to her computer terminal, scanning the reservations for the day. Her instant messenger icon flashed and she clicked on it right away, hoping to see the news she wanted.

Instead, it read 'arrange meeting with Flynn.' This annoyed her. They wanted to know all about the Flynn girl, but couldn't be bothered about her, Delores. Her 'dates' were in exchange for her not-so-ethical services to Montana's goons, yet they'd cancelled on her without a thank you or an apology.

She opened the booking screen and scanned the room assignments. When she saw suite 1004 was vacant, she began to panic. Where was Flynn? Had she checked out? She searched for the surname and found it under 514. Who had made the room change? Marta? She sniffed.

An idea began to form in her head. Since Miss Flynn already occupied a new suite, they wouldn't have any idea that 1004 was vacant until she told them. If they wanted to know her whereabouts so badly, maybe she could set up a surprise for them and get a little revenge in the process.

She typed a one-word reply. 'When.' She stared at the message window, fingers poised over the keyboard. She hit send and waited. Her mind raced ahead, thinking her idea through. They would go to 1004, expecting to meet Flynn. Instead, they'd find her. But what if they spotted Flynn somewhere else in the meantime? Well. Delores would just have to make certain that she wasn't.

The messenger window flashed. 'Weekend. Reply with details, call for escort if necessary.' Delores licked her lips, composed a reply in her mind then typed, 'Understood.' Send. After a moment, the window read 'chat ended.' She exhaled in relief. They were going for it. Now she could work out the details of her little plan.

Linda elbowed her to signal the manager's approach. Delores closed the chat window and returned to the reservation screen. She kept her back to Garcia, the night manager, as he emerged from the back room. She focused on her screen, pretending to be busy. Hopefully he'd ignore her if she ignored him.

"Linda," he said, lingering over the syllables of her name as he wiggled his way behind the counter. A fat, boorish man with greasy hair and bad manners, few of the staff could tolerate Garcia. Fortunately, laziness numbered among his attributes, so while on shift he spent most of his time in the back room eating, watching TV and occasionally checking the security monitors. Empty potato chip bags, candy wrappers and at least three empty cola cans typically remained in his wake. If you wanted to be left alone, a bag of sweets or box of pastries in the back room would make him disappear for hours. Today however, he sidled up to Delores as she scrolled through various screens on her computer.

Leaning in he said, "Good evening, Delores," right in her ear. Too close, he almost made her skin crawl, smelling the sickening combination of hair grease and old-fashioned cologne.

"Sr. Garcia," she said tonelessly, trying to sound professional despite her repulsion.

"I see you've worn my favorite outfit today," he said, peering over her shoulder to get a better look down her unbuttoned shirt. Nauseated, she shifted away from him.

"Just doing my job," she replied, grabbing a handful of tourist brochures to refill the holders on the front desk in an effort to put some distance between them. Garcia backed off.

"And you look very good doing it. Don't forget to run the weekly check-in list. Tomorrow's Friday and a lot of timeshare people will be arriving." With that, he disappeared into the back room again. Delores and Linda exchanged looks, both finding Garcia equally distasteful and went back to work.

*

A few kilometres away from the turnoff to El Mirador,

Cruz concluded that Verrera's plan must be executed without delay, since Verrera himself wouldn't be available while his wife was in hospital.

Hired as Verrera's assistant just six months ago, Bernardo Cruz played the part of an unassuming clerical aide well. He did his paperwork, made phone calls, conducted research. He supposed in a way, that's exactly what he was doing right now. But the work wasn't related to Verrera's day job as the regional development officer. Although Verrera had control over many project approvals, he wanted the one thing his desk job couldn't offer--real wealth.

On the side, Verrera had started up his own contracting business, buying up supposedly unwanted, unviable properties and proposing his own development bids which he could quickly rubber stamp through the approval process. He could then build anything he wanted and reap the rewards of income-generating projects built on real estate bought for next to nothing.

Of course, to keep his government job he couldn't be known as the owner of the new company. A phony front became necessary. Enter Bernardo Cruz.

A man of many talents, Cruz could secure investors. He could acquire business licenses under assumed names. He could remove obstacles that stood in the way of progress. A mysterious man named Salvatore Rodriguez legally owned Verrera's new company, Vistamar Holdings. And the properties it bought were unwanted because Bernardo made them that way.

A prime retail space lay abandoned because of 'structural compromise.' An apartment building in a desirable district suddenly became vacant due to 'pest infestation.' And an old hotel on a deserted strip of beach declared unsafe to rebuild? Sat on an unexpected deposit of bitumen sands, potentially yielding millions of barrels of crude oil once properly extracted.

Verrera had almost cried when Tristan Flynn bought the site, furious that his prize had been taken away from him. Flynn became an obstacle to Vistamar's progress and needed to be removed. Cruz turned out to be very helpful in this regard, too. Yes, Verrera was being clever, but not as clever as his assistant.

Once the projects were underway, Bernardo could pull the rug right out from under Verrera's feet. Because Salvatore Rodriguez was one of Cruz' many aliases. He had collected long ago the necessary credentials to simply appear one day and become Sr. Rodriguez, leaving Verrera out in the cold.

Only one obstacle remained; neither Cruz nor Verrera had counted on the young Miss Flynn becoming involved. No matter, Cruz thought. She could be taken care of just as easily as her father had, if it came to that.

He parked his car at a viewpoint pullout on the main highway. He approached the remains of the building on foot, the sun throwing its' lonely frame into silhouette as it lowered itself to the west. Making poor El Mirador completely undesirable required an additional touch.

The leg bones and ribs from the unfortunate Toro killed last month at Ronda were just the beginning of the scare tactics Cruz had up his sleeve. Posing as an eccentric tourist, he'd talked the local butcher into scraping and drying the bones for him as a souvenir of the spectacular bullfight. They'd made convincing remains of a victim overcome by the quicksand.

But when he followed Flynn's little convoy yesterday, he knew the team would soon discover the quicksand wasn't real. A pocket of bitumen lay close to the surface; no concrete foundation had been poured in that area.

Cruz had done his homework.

Years ago when they found it necessary to expand the original building, the supporting columns had simply been constructed around the troublesome patch of muck. Bernardo discovered that by pumping salt water from the nearby sea underground to the pocket, the sand and oil mixture became 'bloated', losing cohesion and causing the appearance and characteristics of quicksand.

Up to now, the ruse had kept most intruders away. But for Flynn to lose interest in it, El Mirador must die completely. He slunk closer to the columns surrounding the bitumen pocket, carrying his laptop bag. Moving into the shade, he set the bag down carefully and opened it.

He'd removed the computer from the case the night before. Six brick-shaped objects took its place. In another compartment lay a remote device and stubs of wire. He worked efficiently in the shadows, molding the putty-like substance on the surrounding columns and inserting the detonator wires. One more of his many talents--he'd been an army cadet as a young boy and became fascinated with munitions.

A kind of hobby, he learned the history of explosive devices and materials, exactly how they were used and for what purposes. The knowledge came in very handy. By the time he'd finished, the sun dipped below the horizon. He planned to stay until full dusk before leaving.

He sat down in the shade and leaned against a loose block of concrete. He wished he hadn't quit smoking. Now would be a good time for a cigarette, if he weren't surrounded by C-4.

He thought about Michelle and when he would see her Friday night. When he became as rich as he planned to be with Vistamar Holdings, he could have a different partner every night, if he wanted. But none compared to Michelle. He would do almost anything for another tryst with her. As darkness closed in, Bernardo picked up his now empty laptop case and climbed the hill to the viewpoint.

CHAPTER FOURTEEN

Zara enjoyed giving her Spanish a workout in teaming up with Chico. When she couldn't think of the Spanish words she wanted, she threw in a bit of French. Between those two languages and a smattering of English, they communicated well. They seemed to understand exactly what the other wanted to achieve with the project and Zara proved helpful in solving his problem with the exterior detailing.

She volunteered to do the final elevation views and spec out the finishes and materials while he concentrated on the mechanicals. Thanks to the networked computers, she could access Chico's files and work on them in the same CADD program that he used.

She saved the revised files into the proper directories and launched her internet browser to start a search on El Mirador. Her first keyword searches brought up articles on Flynn's purchase of the site. She printed those and tried different keywords to obtain more historical information.

Typing in 'El Mirador Hotel' and 'beach resorts 1960s' returned some interesting photos. At last, she had some images of what the place had looked like and printed those off, too. Alongside the photos were a few entries about the fire, similar to those she'd read before leaving home. She scanned them, noting a repeated name. Businessman and owner Ariel Torres had perished in the incident, leaving no legal will. With no succession plan, no heir apparent, the future of the property remained in limbo. Hmmm. Mr. Smart-Ass had been right.

On a whim, she typed in 'quicksand' to find out more about its composition and where it would be likely to occur. What Ernesto said was true; the sand particles, infused with enough water, separated to the point where friction no longer existed between them to compact and create a solid surface. It would suddenly give way to external pressure and objects exerting that pressure, like a person stepping on it, would sink fast. Hence the term 'quick'.

Even more interesting was the good deal of folklore written about it--how it appeared profusely in stories and movies for a period of time, then became cliché and not used. In addition, the chances of people or animals sinking slowly to their deaths in quicksand appeared to be extremely unlikely, as the quick area was rarely very deep.

A red flag raised in Zara's mind. This could mean the bones they found were not the remains of some unlucky person stepping in the wrong place at the wrong time. They could be, as Dave suggested, a kind of decoy to confuse and deter anyone from discovering the real answers.

She printed off this information as well, then turned her attention to the photographs from the 1950s and early 1960s of the Andalusian coastline. In black and white, the familiar structure of El Mirador appeared clearly in the distance, while period-costumed beachgoers cavorted in the foreground. One photo showed a cigarette billboard, portraying the jet set of the day having a grand time smoking 'El Fresco' menthol cigarettes while enjoying the lifestyle of the Costa del Sol.

The facade of the building screamed 1960s with its diamond-shaped panels in between the rows of windows on each floor. Concrete balconies protruded from beneath every third window, staggered from one row to the next giving it a sort of loose brick patterning. The topmost floor appeared to be a solarium or penthouse ballroom, the windows forming the entire wall. Instead of a typical mid-century commercial flat roof, the glass walls extended upwards in a pyramidal shape, resembling a glass birdcage. The peak converged into a tall spire, with what appeared to be a light beacon at the top.

Overall, an attractive building. Not everyone appreciated the mid-century vogue in architecture. In fact, all over the world great examples of the horizontal and symmetrical stylings of this period had been torn down in favour of new construction. A shame really. Zara believed all period styles were worth preserving. Like people, buildings were a product of their time.

Like people. She decided to research something else. She browsed the news sites using keywords 'Flynn' and 'Jakarta, Indonesia.' Narrowing the results to August of this year, a dozen or so references appeared and she clicked on them one by one. Nothing much new presented itself--the date, the time, the names.

The repetitive journalistic accounts of the incident gnawed at her heart as she read, feeling her dad die again each time the story was retold. All of the reports established the sudden collapse of the partially completed complex and most hinted at faulty materials, worker carelessness or unheeded safety measures. Her face grew hot with anger. Not possible for a project with the Flynn name on it.

Going down the list, the results became more fragmented, less relevant to the hard news listings above. The Spanish excerpts slowed her reading considerably, but one entry stuck out. A local free press publication had a different view, stating in no uncertain terms that the project had been sabotaged as an act of terrorism. The pattern of destruction was consistent with explosive demolition methods. It made special mention of Tristan Benjamin Flynn, CEO of Flynn Enterprises International, stating that Mr. Flynn had been onsite due to a personnel shortage which had put the project behind schedule. Crews were working overtime when the accident occurred at approximately 7:00 p.m. local time.

Zara pressed the print button.

A soft knock sounded on her open office door. Jorge stood there, smiling. "It's five o'clock, Miss. You wish to go back to the hotel now?" She exhaled, realizing she'd just spent her first full day on the job.

"Si, Jorge. It's quitting time," she said, placing her printouts in a neat pile on her desk. She stood up and surveyed the room before leaving. Yes, she really could feel at home here. A big step, leaving Montreal behind and embracing the European lifestyle. It wasn't what she'd planned. She'd pictured herself back in her Westmount condo by Christmas. She would talk with her mother about it when she came. Picking up her bag, she followed Jorge out into the reception area.

Everyone else had left. She cast a thoughtful look down the hall where she'd seen Dave go into his office. "Uh, can you wait just a minute, Jorge?" She went to his door and knocked. No answer. She tried the doorknob and peeked in.

Loads of books lay stacked in neat piles on his drawing table and in orderly rows on shelves. Clean desk except for his laptop, a phone, an inbox, daytimer and pens. Neat freak, she concluded.

In one corner of the office--Zara did a double take--lay several dumbbells of varying weights and a guitar resting in a stand. His framed diplomas hung on the wall next to a Ted Harrison painting. She resisted the urge to check if it was an original or a limited edition. An iconic set of deer antlers were mounted on an adjacent wall and cradled across them, a beat-up hockey stick.

Clearly a multi-faceted individual, this Mr. Parker.

More intrigued than ever, she closed the door and went down to the cool relaxing space of the Mercedes.

"Did you get bored waiting for me?" she asked Jorge as they pulled out into traffic. She had been at work all day and felt badly having him wait around all that time.

"De nada, Miss. I can always find something to do, but I look forward to driving you anywhere you please most of all." She remembered he'd driven Dave back to the office after the site visit yesterday.

"I hope you didn't mind driving Mr. Parker yesterday? I thought it was the least we could do. He missed a day of work to come with us."

"Not at all, Miss. He is a nice boy, very polite." He paused, then added, "Tu le gustas, he likes you, you know."

"Verdad? Really. And how do you know this?" she said, sounding unconvinced. If she didn't know him so well she'd swear Jorge planned to meddle in her personal affairs.

"Lo sé," he said. "I know. The way I know about cars, like this Mercedes. She's a good one." Zara thought about this. Jorge had never been interested in the men in her life before, aside from her father. He'd been like an uncle to her, a familiar comfortable figure that she'd always known.

If what Jorge said was true, how did she feel about Dave? She couldn't deny he was attractive, with his dimpled, boyish good looks and casual style. His six-foot-plus frame moved with an easy grace she found sexy. *But that smart mouth of his.*

He'd invited her out two times now; first for a drink, then to take a ride with him to Gibraltar. If nothing else, he was persistent.

She also thought about Miguel and their crazy rendezvous Tuesday night. The Hispanic Hunk had gotten her mojo going and she didn't seem able to shut it off. She regretted her careless behaviour on that occasion, but secretly wished she could see him again without passing out like a drunken sailor.

Since the chances of that were remote, why not get to know Mr. CET, B.Sc., aka Smart Ass, a little better? Accept his offer? They did have quite a bit in common. But she'd made plans with the Ridleys and didn't want to duck out on them.

Perhaps she could find a way to meet him 'accidentally' in Gibraltar. She would talk to Bette and Diggy tonight. Having dinner with them had become a bit of a routine. She enjoyed their company, like going to a favorite relative's house for Thanksgiving.

"He does seem like a very trustworthy person," Zara said, not wanting to give Jorge any further ideas about playing matchmaker. They drove back to Marbella in silence.

When they arrived back at the Club, Zara saw one of the desk clerks, a girl with huge boobs, waving at her and beckoning her to the desk. Thinking there must be a message from the Ridleys, she walked over.

"Miss Flynn, I have message for you!" she said with excitement.

"Yes?"

"The manager wants to give you a complimentary gift, for the inconvenience of changing rooms. We are sorry you were unhappy with the first one."

"That's quite alright, Marta took care of the switch. There's no need for a gift."

"Gracias, Miss. But we want our guests to be very *very* happy with our resort, so this is for you." She handed Zara an envelope. She opened it and withdrew a gift certificate. A cable car tour of Gibraltar and a one-night stay at a place called the Aragon Pub and Hotel. What a coincidence! The tour was for up to four people. She could treat Bette and Diggy in appreciation for being so nice to her.

"Gracias," she said to Delores. "Is it valid on the weekend?" Delores' smile wavered a little.

"It is only good for Friday, tomorrow," she said. "I hope that is satisfactory. Can I call and make the reservation for you?"

"Um, I would like to invite some friends, let me check with them first," Zara said.

"No problema, Miss. Please call the front desk when you are ready, I will be here all evening," Delores said. Zara smiled and nodded, holding up the envelope.

"Thank you again," she said.

When Zara got to 514, she dialed the Ridley's room. Bette answered.

"Hi Bette, it's Zara."

"Oh, Zara dear, so nice to hear from you. Did you have a nice day at the office?"

"I did," she said. "The people are so nice and I got to work on some projects right away. I think I'm going to like it there."

"Aww, that's terrific, luv. Are you up for dinner tonight? Dig and me is just thinking about going to the seafood place instead of the hotel dining room. You fancy lobster or sommat, dear?"

"Sounds great, Bette. And I have some good news, you still want to go to Gib this weekend?"

"Of course, luv. It's one of our favorite places, just like back home. Can you come with us?"

"I'll do better than that. I have a gift certificate for a tour and overnight stay tomorrow. Would that work for you?"

"Brilliant!" Bette said. "Dig, we've got a tour and an overnight in Gib," Zara heard her say off-line to Diggy. "Tomorrow's fine, luv. Can you tear yourself away from work? We should make a day of it. You'll love it there."

"I think I can swing that," Zara said with a laugh. "I'm the boss, after all." Bette giggled.

"Smashing, dear. We'll talk about it over dinner. Meet you downstairs in an hour?"

"I'll be there," Zara said and hung up.

CHAPTER FIFTEEN

Miguel Montana, international superstar and Latin singing sensation, lay soaking in a bubble bath in the penthouse suite of Club Marbella. His own music played loudly throughout the room as he laid his head back on the little bath pillow with his eyes closed, listening intently to his performance on the recording.

He had one more show to do here Saturday night, so he reviewed the last show's sound files as he always did, noting the crowd reaction, backup band sound and other elements in order to make changes or improvements.

Whatever else he might be, Miguel was a consummate performer, devoting himself fully to his art, his music. He thanked God for his life and livelihood. He loved nothing better than to sing, except perhaps to compose new music. These talents were gifts and being raised Spanish Catholic, he of course knew these things came from God.

He was aware that many called him "Mickey Mountain," the literal English translation of his name, which seemed to amuse the Brits. It inferred him being built as big as a mountain in certain places. But he never gave much thought as to whether he was large, small or average in that department, content in his belief that he was exactly as God intended him to be.

A simple wooden crucifix hung above the tub, while creamy-white pillar candles burned on the ledge all around. After bathing he would say a prayer, give thanks for his last show and ask a blessing for success with the next one.

He listened to the closing number, smiling at the sound of his last note and the screaming of the crowd in approval. Not a thing he would change, he concluded. One of his best performances.

He 'd been inspired when he saw the beautiful lady he had met in the elevator sitting in the crowd. Normally the stage lights were too bright to see the audience, but at that moment he happened to be standing at just the right mark, between the spotlights crossbeam, to see her.

Miguel took this as a sign that she was someone special and that he should select her as the one to share himself with that night. If he loved anything as much as his music, it was love itself. He loved everything about his life and he viewed it as a personal tribute to his gifts, to make love to someone each night of his touring engagements as the ultimate expression of thanks for his talent and good fortune.

However, his interpretation of his faith's concept of universal love extended to more than just women. He loved all people, men and women and celebrated this idea of interconnectedness by swinging both ways in his desires.

Miss Red Dress, as he'd first dubbed her, was as sweet and fresh as he'd imagined when Luis and Raoul, his personal bodyguards, had brought her to the penthouse. Already drunk, she carried herself with aplomb nevertheless. He thought speaking French a nice touch. It made him feel like he'd taken them both to a special, private place for just the two of them to share an intimate connection.

He didn't know she would react badly to the tranquilizer

in her water. A mild substance, he often used it to cloud his partner's memory a little. That way, most of them didn't remember enough to make an issue of it to the police or their lawyers, or anyone else. It all seemed like a pleasantly erotic dream.

Occasionally though, he took regular lovers of both sexes. Typically these were people of use to him, that helped him acquire other, more transient partners in his travels. The lovely Miss Zara Flynn for example. She'd been procured by faithful Delores, his main contact here at the Club Marbella where he toured once or twice a year. In exchange for her services, Miguel would often 'service' her, just the way she liked it.

Delores had a thing for role-playing and costumes. She loved being someone else and would delight Miguel with a new guise each time they met in secret. And oh, those magnificent, cantaloupe-sized breasts! He licked his lips just picturing them in his mind, stroking their round firmness, feeling the weight of them in his hands.

The places they met were arousing too--the hidden storage room, in particular--provided a wicked, forbidden atmosphere of secrecy that Miguel found amusing. Thankfully, Delores had been kind enough to help Miss Flynn into bed after she'd passed out. But as much as he appreciated Delores, he didn't feel guilty in the least about standing her up. He'd received a better offer.

It didn't matter as long as he delivered his gift of lovemaking while he was on the road, and Delores would come running back to him another time as she always did. He didn't often get to experience the kind of scenario he had last night. He smiled thinking about it. The element of danger and decadence his Ángel Oscuro offered, his Dark Angel, was irresistible. He accepted it as a challenge to his expression of universal love, to mix male and female when presented with the opportunity and so he opted to be with Ángel instead of Delores.

Ángel wanted to see him again on Friday and for the moment, he'd agreed.

He also hoped to resume his meeting with Zara before the tour ended. He remembered cupping her smooth buttocks in his hand, preparing to give her such pleasure when she slumped to the floor, unconscious.

Luis knocked at the bathroom door. "Message coming in from the front desk. Friday night, 9:00 o'clock, in 1004. I should accept?" Miguel smoothed the fragrant bathwater over his face with both hands, the wet curls of his hair sticking to his handsome face.

"Por supuesto, Luis. Of course," he said, wiggling his toes beneath the bubbles. Ángel would just have to understand. Mickey Mountain would have his second chance at Miss Red Dress.

*

Ignacio sat in the hospital waiting room cradling a cold, bitter-tasting coffee in a styrofoam cup between his hands. He'd been here more than 24 hours since Carmella had collapsed in their kitchen yesterday. He didn't know what to do. His sister had taken the girls to her house for a few days, the poor things. They were upset and frightened.

Why must Carmella always be so critical of him? He made a good living, had given her a home and family and now when on the verge of success with his new company, she lay in this place, fighting for her life and blaming him for everything. It wasn't fair. He deserved better than this. He almost hoped she might not pull through, thus ending his misery in trying to please her and impress his father-in-law.

He shook his head to cast the thought from his mind. That would leave his girls without a mother. How could he entertain such an idea? Her inheritance would pass down to Daniela and Ericka in that case. They would be set for life.

If he could just get Vistamar Holdings to pay off as big as he hoped he could buy himself a completely new life, including a new wife. The country had no shortage of gold-digging, self-centered women who wanted nothing more than to lie on the beach and have a rich husband support them. The crazy idea swirled and formed in his mind until he felt dizzy, almost nauseous.

He realized he hadn't eaten since lunchtime yesterday, but couldn't bring himself to take a meal. Surely not hospital food in any case. His cell phone began to vibrate--such devices weren't to be switched on while in hospital, so he'd set it on silent. He fished it out of his shirt pocket and read the screen. Cruz was calling. This brought him back to reality and to the problem of El Mirador. "Si," he answered.

"How is your wife?" came the response.

"I'm not sure," he confided to his assistant. "The doctors, they don't tell me much. Just that she is under observation."

"I'm sorry to hear that. You are under a lot of strain, are you going to be alright?"

"Bernardo, I'm not sure about anything right now. Are you at the office?"

"No. I've let them know I'll be there in the morning. I took the afternoon to... move forward with Vistamar." Ignacio brightened.

"What is the status?" he asked.

"The fire is in the hole," Bernardo replied. "I can pull the trigger at any time. Since you are indisposed, I felt we should move ahead sooner rather than later. I may not have time to watch Flynn's movements and cover for you at the office as well. There's no reason to wait."

"Very well. When will you do it?"

"This weekend. I'll let you know. Stay with your wife, it will make a good alibi." Ignacio nodded in agreement.

"Bernardo, I don't believe I have thanked you for your services." Verrera said, emotionally and physically drained.

Bernardo sounded surprised at this uncharacteristic sentiment. "De nada, Sr. Verrera. It is what you pay me for."

"You are assuming great risk. You will be fairly compensated, believe me. Like you were in Indonesia."

"That was incidental and in the past. I look to the future, as should you," Bernardo said, changing the subject. He evidently didn't want to review that event.

"Por supuesto. Of course, Bernardo. Keep me appraised." He disconnected. He could tell Cruz did not want to talk about Indonesia. His work there took a different twist than intended, but what was done was done.

When Tristan Flynn's purchase trumped Vistamar's bid for the El Mirador site, Verrera nearly lost his mind. He sent Cruz to Indonesia, the site of Flynn's new build in central Java. Before he knew it, Flynn was dead, caught in the explosion of his own project.

He'd intended only to destroy the building, to make Flynn reconsider his purchase of El Mirador and divert funds to the Indonesian venture. But the man had been where he shouldn't have and suffered the consequences. This led to his daughter's presence here and a new obstacle to his plans.

He tried not to think about the dark turn his new company had taken. Soon, it would be over and Vistamar would emerge as brightly as the sun, fueling his new destiny. He crushed the now-empty styrofoam cup and tossed it into a nearby wastebasket. *I must talk to the doctors,* he thought. *It has been too long without information*. He needed to know whether his wife would be part of his future or not. He started down the hall to the nurses station.

Chapter Sixteen

An ordinary Canadian kid, David Justin Parker had no idea what he wanted to be when he grew up. He'd spent his youth in ordinary Canadian fashion, loving the outdoors, going to the lake on summer vacations with his family and partying with his high school friends.

He bought his first car at 17, saving up money from part-time jobs at gas stations, restaurants and retail stores. While working at a building supply centre he discovered a love of the construction trades. Math and Science came easily to him and he had no difficulty gaining entrance to Lakehead University in Thunder Bay. After two years there he applied to the prestigious Massachusetts Institute of Technology and was accepted. After graduation he scored his job with Flynn Enterprises in Boston. At the age of 27 he now lived in Spain, supervising construction projects all over the Andalusian coast.

He thought he'd done pretty well for himself and his family back in Thunder Bay took great pride in him. He pounded up the steps from the waterfront to the bike path on the causeway. Only a few blocks from his apartment now, he'd nearly finished his usual 3km morning run. He passed the familiar office towers and commercial buildings of downtown Malaga. He could still glimpse the sea beyond their concrete and glass silhouettes.

What a view. He felt lucky to have ridden his career to this beautiful place in life. The Costa del Sol teemed with exciting nightlife, great cuisine, stunning beaches and even more stunning women. In the three years he'd been here, he'd met dozens, dated several and slept with one or two.

In fact, he'd recently broken it off with a certain auburn-haired esthetician whose painful obsession with looks took on literal meaning when she'd insisted on waxing him within an inch of his life. The rest were equally superficial. He couldn't say he'd been in love with any of them. He'd certainly never spoken the words.

Now this Montrealer had breezed into his life and made him realize something. That he missed home and the kind of girlfriends he'd known in his youth. The kind who made the volleyball team, weren't afraid to dive off the dock, bait a hook or chug a beer.

More than that, she made his heart ache with a nagging question. How would she feel if she knew her father went to Indonesia because of him?

He checked his watch. 7:45 a.m. He'd told her to call by 8 if she was interested in coming along to Gibraltar today. He found himself feeling anxious, knowing he'd be disappointed if she didn't call.

God, she turned him on.

He'd kept his cell phone clipped to his shorts while he ran, just in case. He slowed his pace as he reached the steps to his apartment building and went inside. Opening the door to his third floor apartment he took out his cell phone and looked for missed calls. Nothing. *Did I offend her that much?* She puzzled him. Normally people flocked to him, not eyed him up and down as if he were the village bum. He wasn't used to being...*rejected?* Huh. That word didn't exist in his lexicon.

He set the phone down and stripped, heading for the shower. His voicemail would pick up the message anyway and he wouldn't feel like he was waiting on her call if he just got on with things. If she did call, he'd have her number and an excuse to call back.

Showered, dressed and ready by 8:15, his cell phone sat where he'd left it on the coffee table, undisturbed and unblinking. He shoved it in his pocket, grabbed his file box of work orders and left the apartment. *Just another lonely day in paradise*.

*

Ernesto's cell phone rang. When he picked up, he heard Zara's voice on the other end. "Buenas días, my dear. Como esta?"

"Good morning, Ernesto. Muy bien, gracias. I was wondering. Mr. Parker mentioned he might go to Gibraltar today. Do you know what suppliers he planned to visit?"

Ernesto thought for a moment. "Well, he normally visits the shipping office at the harbour. I think he also had some safety supply orders coming in, that would be at Prof International, in downtown Gibraltar. Why do you ask?"

"I planned to come in to the office again today, but an opportunity's come up to treat some friends of mine to a tour in Gibraltar. I thought if Mr. Parker would be there, I might invite him to dinner with us, to thank him for his help. It *is* Friday, so..."

"That's very thoughtful of you, Zara," Ernesto said. I'm sure he'd love to join you. Why don't I give you his cell number, you can catch up with him between appointments."

"That's okay Ernie, I have his card. I want to surprise him. Thanks. See you Monday!"

Alvarez hung up the phone and smiled. It seemed he wouldn't have to work that hard to interest these two young people in each other after all. He'd purposely chosen Dave to lead the site visit and wanted to keep him and Zara working together. He hadn't been entirely truthful when he'd told Zara he had no insight into her father's thoughts. The last time they'd seen each other, Tristan said to him:

"Ernie, I have a lovely, talented, strong-willed daughter who needs to find more than just a career. If she would just come and work for me, she could have this office, spend weekends on the beach and have a little romance for a change. I don't know what it would take to make her change her mind."

Ernesto thought of Zara. She *was* lovely. She *was* talented. He found it difficult to look at her without seeing Marlena. But she had a career and now the responsibilities of Flynn Enterprises as well. For a girl like her, the only way to grant Tristan's wish was to provide work and romance in the same place.

That's where David came in.

Aside from the fact that he liked him, Ernesto knew that Dave was single, a truly good man and an attractive one, according to some of the office girls. They called him 'El semental Canadiense' behind his back. The Canadian stud.

Certain that Dave had no idea he was being 'fixed up,' Ernesto wanted to keep it that way. His smile grew a little wider. Tristan would have been pleased.

*

The rising sun turned up the heat on the beaches of the Costa del Sol. Zara felt totally carefree today, racing down the coastal highway with Jorge at the wheel of the Mercedes and her 'foster' parents Bette and Digbert Ridley in the back seat. It felt like a vacation now, with nothing more pressing on her schedule than sightseeing and shopping.

"Well, first we've got to take the cable car up the Rock," Bette said. "Did you know there was monkeys living up in them cliffs there? It's true! Then we'll have a right nice lunch and hit the shops for the afternoon. We'll watch the sunset from the harbour and have a slap-up night in the pub." Bette seemed to have everything under control, as usual. Diggy sat silent, humoring her and enjoying the view out the car window.

Even on this bright day, Zara felt anxiety building as they neared the turn off at El Mirador. This time she could drive right by it and not concern herself with it for the moment. There was no other route to Gibraltar. But the problem remained in the back of her mind. It would be a huge undertaking. Would it be worth it? She remembered the photographs she'd collected. Perhaps she shouldn't try and resurrect the dead-- leave its' memory be. But left unrestored it would have to be taken down. It presented an ecological hazard. And still, there must be a reason her father had given it to her. There was more to the story, she could feel it.

But she didn't want to solve mysteries today.

Today she would enjoy with her new friends and if luck prevailed, a certain special friend. The hills to the north began to flatten and soon their route passed through a plainlike region, creating a wide horizon before them. Out of the haze to the west, the Rock began to reveal itself. Even in the distance, the distinctive shape of Gibraltar was awe-inspiring. It looked exactly like every photo or drawing ever made of it and it grew larger and more solid with each passing kilometre.

Jorge reminded them they would require their passports to cross La Linea, the border between Spain and Great Britain. When they arrived at the crossing, the Rock of Gibraltar's imposing silhouette seemed to fill the sky.

They entered the territory on foot. A car wasn't necessary and Jorge had other plans for the day. His half-sister Elena and her children were meeting him at Bermuda Beach, a few miles east of La Linea. He would return for them tomorrow.

They bid him goodbye at the base, Gibraltar being home to a major British military installation. Its' airport formed a kind of 'no man's land' between the two countries. The path from the parking lot to the border station ran alongside outbuildings, barracks and parked aircraft belonging to the British Navy.

With the temperature rising and no shade to speak of while traversing the base, Zara worried about Bette and Diggy walking that distance in the hot sun. Bette assured her they were quite used to this trip, having been here many times.

With their passports stamped at the entry point, they continued down Winston Churchill Avenue into the town of Gibraltar.

They found the cable car station, bought their tickets and went across the street to a charming old coffee shop before taking the seven-minute ride to the top. Done up in a faux Tudor front, a pair of iron coach lanterns decorated either side of its painted entrance door.

They bought their coffees and pastry and selected a table by the leaded-glass front windows to sit and chat. Bette and Diggy seemed right at home in the little English-style room. Bette identified the rustic country print on the tablecloths as a 'toile' pattern. They sipped hot coffee and talked about life in England. The Ridleys loved their vacations, but always looked forward to returning to the gray skies and changing seasons of the British Isles.

"We was born there, and we'll be planted there," Diggy stated firmly. They took turns asking Zara questions about her personal life. Did she have a boyfriend back home, would she stay in Spain for a while or return to life in Montreal. And what about children, did she like children?

"Wait a minute. What's with the interrogation?" Zara

asked. "I've told you most everything about me, why so many questions?"

"We's just interested, dear. Our Jamie's long grown now, moved off to Scotland raising his prize piglets on a farm there. Don't suppose he'll ever get married, he's happy enough on his own. And what lass would be interested in pig farming eh, I ask you?" Bette continued.

"Dibbs out." Zara said. Bette shook her curly hair and laughed.

"Oh, no dear. You're hardly Jamie's type," she said, taking a sip of her coffee. "But you must have plans for a family someday? Pity Mickey Mountain's not available eh…he'd make good breeding stock and all!" she added with a wink.

Zara clapped a hand to her forehead.

"Puh-lease, Bette, enough of Mickey Mountain! It's embarrassing enough as it is. And I haven't seen 007 or 008 lurking around anywhere, so I think I'm safe. Let's drop it." Bette eased up, set her cup down on its saucer and peered out the window to watch the cable car loading and unloading at the base station.

"Like they say, the right guy will come along. I'm in no hurry," Zara said. "And I do like children, to answer your question." Diggy patted her arm.

"And a great mam you'll make someday, too. No need rushing things now is there?" They finished their coffee and moments later were rising up the slope of The Rock.

The views of the Mediterranean were incredible and to the west, the Alborean Sea. Beyond that, the open Atlantic beckoned. The interactive tour guide rambled through its' spiel, pointing out the flora and fauna along the way with tidbits of history thrown in. There were indeed wild monkeys, called Barbary Apes, in the area as Bette had said. However, none of them seemed amenable to making an appearance today.

They reached the summit and disembarked, everyone gasping "oohs" and "aahs" and pulling out cameras and binoculars to capture the view. The misty African coast, visible on a clear day like today--took Zara's breath away.

They browsed in the gift shop, trying to avoid the touristy trinkets, but Diggy emerged from the shop sporting a hat with "Gibraltar Rocks!" embroidered on the brim. Bette chose a whisky flask shaped like the Rock and Zara found a lime-green chiffon scarf with metallic threads woven into tiny tassels at the ends. She wrapped it stylishly around her neck. It set off her eyes and went beautifully with the emerald green sundress she wore.

She posed with Bette for Diggy to take a photo, the blue sea at their backs and the imposing peak of the Rock looming to one side.

They had fun behaving like tourists, snapping photos and strolling through the botanic gardens. Then it was back down the mountain for lunch. Diggy insisted on going to a traditional English-style pub, to show Zara what proper fish and chips tasted like.

As they walked down the street near the harbour, Bette and Diggy stopped to look in the window of a pawn shop. Seeing something of interest, they went in to check out the merchandise. Zara followed them, assuming that it probably took one junk shop owner to know another.

In the cluttered interior she saw everything from can openers to camo wear, TVs to tumble dryers. It smelled faintly of kerosene and a thin layer of dust covered most everything. Lamps and wind chimes hung from the ceiling. They tinkled unrhythmically as she made her way to the back counter where the Ridleys huddled over something along with the proprietor.

As she came within a few feet of the group Bette straightened, slinging an antique rifle expertly in her arms, peering through the sight and checking the bolt action of the piece.

Zara recoiled involuntarily.

Bette set the rifle back down on the counter. "It's decent, not sure we need another one of them. How about the Colt, then?" The proprietor showed her a classic handgun next, which Bette picked up and examined in a similar manner to the rifle. "We'll come back later, if we're interested," she said.

She and Diggy turned to leave and saw the dumbstruck Zara standing there. "Oh, Zara dear, I suppose we've given you a fright! You look positively gob-smacked...so sorry, did we mention that's one of our shop specialties back home?"

"Just a hobby line, really," Diggy said. "Collector items mostly, anything related to the Empire's military history."

"Guns?" Zara said, barely managing to speak. "You sell guns in your curiosity shop?" Bette waved her hand nonchalantly.

"Collector pieces," she affirmed. "No ammo."

"Bette's a crack shot though. Get her to the skeet range and look out," Diggy quipped, tapping Bette on the backside as he passed her on his way to the door.

"Oh, give over. I haven't done that in years," she said, following him. Zara stayed frozen to the spot. When they noticed she wasn't in step with them, they turned around to see the shocked, blank expression on her face.

Bette let out a laugh. "Come along lass, you look as though you need a stiff drink!"

"We're harmless, really," added Diggy. They each linked an arm with Zara and led her out of the shop. "Ah, here's the Mucky Duck," he announced after they had walked a few blocks.

The old style pub sign hung out on a wrought-iron frame. 'The Black Swan,' it read in bold curvaceous letters, a dark silhouette of the bird painted beneath them. Zara got the joke.

Familiar with Cockney slang which nicknamed things and places with rhyming synonyms, "Mucky" meant Black, and "Duck" instead of Swan.

They went inside and settled into a red stuffed-vinyl booth nestled under a large window. Lacy curtains trimmed with black pompoms hung above it. Wall sconces flickered with candlelight and dark papered walls sported a traditional Tudor plank moulding. Zara found the whole place charming right down to the unfinished wood floor, scuffed and distressed to perfection.

Diggy ordered pints for all three of them. It felt good to get out of the heat and sip a cool beer in the cozy darkness of the pub. Diggy also insisted on the fish and chips and in no time, a huge platter of steaming hot fillets and newspaper-lined baskets of fried potatoes appeared on their table.

Bette doused the chips with vinegar and squeezed lemon wedges over the fish. The mouth-watering aroma overshadowed the fact that the fare was loaded with innumerable amounts of fat and calories. No one could resist the greasy, battery goodness that lay before them.

"Tuck in, ladies," Diggy said.

As a second round of pints arrived, Zara looked out the window to admire the view of the harbour. Across the street amid the collection of jewellery shops and camera stores stood the harbour control office. As she squinted to read the lettering on the door, it swung open. In the back of her mind, she'd hoped to spot him somewhere today and here he was, stepping right in to view.

Dave Parker came out of the harbour office, his head turned in conversation with the man following him out the door. Waving a goodbye, Dave headed across the street towards the Black Swan, looking like a man with a thirst on.

Zara watched him cross the street, wearing sunglasses, steel-toed work boots, jeans and white tee underneath an unbuttoned cotton shirt. He looked both ways as he crossed to the pub, his long, lean legs carrying him in a casual but purposeful stride, like an athlete. He stepped up to the door and took off his sunglasses before entering the darkened establishment.

A few heads turned to see the newcomer, including Bette's.

She looked Dave up and down, then turned back to the table. "Ooh, who's this then?" she said in a sly tone. "He's a right looker, eh?"

Zara smirked, undecided on how long she would let things go before revealing that she knew the handsome stranger. "You think he's good-looking, Bette?" she asked casually, swirling the dregs of her pint around in its mug.

"What, not your type, luv?" Bette asked. "The hot sun must have boiled your brain if you don't think he's a nice bit of stuff." Diggy rolled his eyes in his long-suffering manner. It seemed his wife would never quit being so outspoken.

Dave took a seat at the bar with his back to them. The landlord saw to his order and began pulling a pint from the tap.

Well, he did offer to buy me a drink the other day, perhaps I can return the favour, Zara thought. She excused herself from the table despite Bette's objection that she should get her second pint down her. "I have to make a visit," she whispered, pointing to the washrooms.

Instead, she approached Dave's chair from behind. He sat with his elbows on the bar, reading a local newspaper. She took the seat next to him, mimicking his body position. The landlord returned with his pint and Zara spoke up. "I'll get that," she said and slid a fiver of the local currency, Gibraltar pounds, across to the barkeep.

Dave raised his head, stared straight ahead for a split second then turned toward her. His face displayed a priceless mix of shock and delight. "What are you doing here?" were the first words from his lips.

"You might say thank you," she said, pointing to his foaming pint of beer.

"Thank you," he echoed. He stared at her for a few seconds then burst into a full-on smile. With his dimples and sparkling white teeth showing, the pub no longer seemed dark. Zara couldn't help but smile back.

She watched his eyes travel down the length of her body. Aware of her short skirt, she crossed her legs, a bit á la Sharon Stone, and tilted her ankle up and down. The tiny rhinestones on her sandal strap glinted in the muted light.

He swallowed hard and reached for his pint, as if suddenly thirstier than he'd realized. "I thought you would call me for a ride," he said. "How did you get here?"

Zara cocked her head in the direction of Bette and Diggy. "I told you I had some friends who wanted to take a trip here. That's Mr. & Mrs. Ridley, from Liverpool." Dave turned to look in the direction she indicated. Bette and Diggy stared at them from their table by the window, Diggy smiling broadly and Bette's eyes practically spinning around in her head. Dave nodded and waved. They waved back absently, appearing confounded at this new turn of events.

He turned back to Zara. "They seem a little old for you."

Zara laughed. "They kind of adopted me on my first day here. I wanted to treat them to a day out."

"I see," Dave said. "And how's the day been so far?"

"We've been up the Rock already, and took a ton of pictures. After lunch we plan to hit the shops. Any recommendations?"

"I thought shopping wasn't your thing," Dave said, taking a sip of his pint. Zara looked him straight in the eye.

"I lied."

Dave's eyebrows went up as he leaned his head forward in a suspicious nod. "Well, like I said, I mostly hang out in lumberyards," he said. "But if you just head down Main Street you'll find a lot of designer shops and jewellery stores."

"Thanks for the tip. Care to join me?" she asked.

"Oh, I wouldn't want to tear you away from your adoptive parents," he said. The barkeep returned with a pint for Zara.

"Oh, I have one going over at…" She gestured to the table by the window. Already making a fast exit, Diggy sent her a mock salute and Bette waved her hands toward her in a 'carry on' motion. They'd sent her pint over with the barkeep.

"We'll see you at the Aragon, dear. Have fun!" Bette said loudly.

As they bustled out the door, Dave said, "I think you've been booted out of the nest. Time to try your wings."

Zara felt a little guilty ditching them, but inwardly grateful to have some time alone with Dave. The intensity of emotion she felt in his presence surprised her. A fine line existed between wanting to be near him and wanting to take revenge on him for all his snide remarks. They finished their pints and Dave ordered another along with the famous fish and chips. Zara opted for a Margarita.

"Your poison of choice, Tequila…?" he asked.

She brushed the salted rim of the glass with her finger and then licked the stray crystals off the tip. "Oh, I think there are worse poisons," she said after a pause. She rubbed the tip of her finger against her tongue and glanced sideways at him. "Like workplace relationships."

Dave pursed his lips in a silent whistle. "Poison indeed. The Devil's water." He studied her with the concentration deserving of a complicated building tender.

Seeing she had his full attention, Zara took an anticipatory first sip of her drink and swallowed appreciatively. "Mmm… yeah." She bobbed her head in a slow nod, tracing her tongue across her upper lip. He'd quoted a song lyric. She recalled the words and spoke them aloud. "The devil's water it ain't so sweet…" she paused, "…but you don't have to drink right now." She flashed him a sweet smile.

His eyes glittered while he appeared to assess her words and work out the next line. "But you can dip your feet?" he said.

He'd caught on. Zara nodded. *Good Lord, I'm flirting like a call girl.* It occurred to her the song was done by *The Killers.* How appropriate.

He let out a sharp laugh as if to snap her spell over him. He looked away, focusing on his pint mug and sliding his fingers up and down the wet glass. "Coming from lake country I've always favoured jumping straight in," he said.

"Oh. To get it over with?"

"No, to enjoy the experience as long as possible." He tore a small chunk of fish from the steaming fillet on his plate and popped it in his mouth.

"Most people like to know what they're getting into before they jump," Zara said.

He swallowed his fish and washed it down with a gulp of beer before stealing a sidelong glance at her. "I already know what I want to get into."

Zara's mouth dropped open a little. His boldness didn't seem to have many boundaries. And despite being taken aback, she had to admit this trait held a roguish charm. They lingered at the bar, exchanging double-entendres over a second margarita and two Spanish coffees.

Dave checked his watch. "Uh-oh. It's nearly two. I still have a few stops to make. Do you want me to give you a lift over to Main Street?"

Zara felt pleasantly lubricated. "Not really. Mind if I tag along with you?" she said.

The same enigmatic half-smile from yesterday crept across Dave's face as he rose from his barstool. He reached for her hand to help her down. "Okay, but I warn you, it might be boring. Are you sure?"

She accepted his hand and slid off the stool. "I'll risk it," she said, looking deeply into those blue eyes.

CHAPTER SEVENTEEN

Bernardo squirmed uncomfortably in his office chair. By four o'clock, he'd done just about all the paperwork and phone calls he could stand for one day in Verrera's absence and his anxiety level climbed higher by the minute. Business waited to be taken care of in Marbella. And so did Michelle.

He had a difficult time keeping his mind off her and the prospect of seeing her again tonight, as they'd planned. But, first things first. He needed to get back to the Club to keep an eye on Miss Flynn and her cohorts. Certain things had to be done that would not be served by sitting here in the Malaga office. He decided to call it a day.

The shadows lengthened in the late afternoon sun and the temperature dropped just enough to make the drive back to the Club enjoyable. Bernardo again put the top down on his convertible, feeling the wind swirl around him as he drove faster and faster. He didn't care about the speed limit, such as there was. The sound system on full, he grooved to a lively salsa track and pushed the accelerator all the way down. Victory dangled almost within reach and he couldn't wait to take it.

In his room, he pulled off his shirt and tie and turned on

the shower. As he undressed, he took a long look at himself in the mirror. The reflection of a skinny man with a heavy five o'clock shadow, shaven head and protruding ears stared back.

His best feature, he decided, were his eyes. Deep brown. So dark a shade that his pupils were barely distinguishable from the iris surrounding them. They filled nearly all of the visible area of his eyes, showing very little of the whites. Someone once told him his eyes were like those of a mouse. But he didn't care. He thought the darkness of his eyes made him look worldly and mysterious.

He admired the small tattoo on his chest, over his heart. A tiny figure with wings, all in black ink. The lettering above it read 'Ángel' and below it, 'Oscuro.' The Dark Angel. The same winged figure appeared on the back of his left hand. He turned and stepped into the shower to get ready for the evening.

*

Friday afternoons were always busy at Club Marbella's front desk. Delores and Marta both worked at top speed to accommodate all the timeshare check-ins. Taxis and airport shuttles seemed to arrive every few minutes. As they coded cardkeys and entered information into the reservation system, Delores' shift passed quickly. At 5:45 she had just enough time to file all the paperwork and tidy up for the next clerks on shift at 6:00.

She had big plans for this evening, even if her 'date' didn't know it. She'd used the master cardkey earlier that afternoon to make some final touches to room 1004. She ordered roses from the floral shop on the mezzanine and set a bottle of champagne to chill in the bar fridge. An assortment of bath oils and fizzy bombs lay in a tray on the tub ledge and candles of all shapes and sizes filled the room.

Almost ready to leave, Delores quickly launched her instant

messenger. As expected, her contacts were online ready for messages at any time. 'Keys at drop location 9pm' she typed, hitting enter to send the message. '9 pm confirmed' came the reply. She ended the chat and logged off.

All set, she thought, proud of herself and her clever machinations. A stroke of genius, the gift certificate would guarantee the relatively flat-chested Zara Flynn to be out of the picture for the night. Delores would be the one getting all the rewards she deserved in suite 1004 tonight. Excited just thinking about it, she hurried to the staff lounge to change.

*

Ignacio Verrera stood in the hospital ward talking to Dr. Rojas, the cardiologist. "She is very lucky," the doctor said. "Many heart attack victims die from the first onset. But your wife is responding well to treatment and there is no significant damage…this time. The best advice is to reduce stress and follow a healthier diet. I recommend you see the nutritionist before Mrs. Verrera is discharged."

"When will she be able to come home?" Ignacio asked.

"I would like her to stay one more night for observation, so in the morning would be best. We have reduced staff on the weekends, so she may get better rest at home."

"Thank you, doctor," he said as they parted ways, Dr. Rojas returning to the nurses station down the hall and Ignacio walking the few steps to Carmella's room. He entered quietly and stood by the bedside, watching the rise and fall of her chest, her head turned to one side and hands folded on top of the coverlet. The cardiac monitor beeped and showed a steady readout. Fatigue washed over him.

Tomorrow they would be back home and the girls could return from his sisters'. But would things be the same? He thought not. He might have to hire some domestic help for awhile, until Carmella recovered. And how would she feel about him now, after the argument they had? He felt sure she would blame him for her heart attack, that her frustration at his inadequacy caused her condition.

He thought about what Bernardo had said too, that the time for action was now. He must acquire El Mirador as soon as possible and approve the development plans. The sooner it produced valuable fossil fuel, the sooner he'd be a very rich man.

Carmella began to stir. Her fingers twitched and she moved her head from side to side. Ignacio took hold of her hand and stroked her forehead with the other. The tight curly strands of her black hair stuck to her face and he brushed them away gently.

"Cariña." Her eyes fluttered open and she gaped at him for a short moment, as if not recognizing him. Then her gaze softened and her lips tried to form words. "You don't have to speak," he said gently. "Just rest."

Her right hand shook as she placed it overtop of his. Her eyes focused fully on him now, the look in them one of faith and forgiveness. *Perhaps all was not lost.*

*

The quiet streets lay darkened as the sun set behind the great Rock. The couple walked unhurried down the cobblestone lane that led to the Aragon Pub and Hotel. The sound of their steps against the stone echoed in the narrow lane. His arm loosely around her shoulders, hers encircled around his waist. To a passerby, they might have been two people who'd known each other a lifetime, but in truth had only met two days ago.

Against her better judgement, Zara knew she was falling for this man. They'd spent the remainder of the afternoon finishing Dave's errands, then window shopping along Main street, occasionally stopping inside a shop that sold gemstones, watches, or books. With no end of interesting buildings in

Gibraltar, of different centuries and cultures, they admired and critiqued them with their combined knowledge of architecture and engineering as they walked leisurely through the town.

Mr. Smart-Ass seemed to disappear when he really got into a topic of interest to him. His speech became animated and his voice filled with an infectious enthusiasm as he expounded the virtues of arch construction or cantilevered beams. Sharing their common passions made her feel drawn to him in a way she hadn't experienced with anyone else.

They walked the last few blocks along the narrow, steep streets to the Aragon.

"Have you worked up an appetite for dinner yet?" he asked her. She looked down at their feet stepping slowly in time with each other, his workboots next to her dainty sandals. Even in her heels, he stood at least a head taller and Zara felt safe, locked in his embrace as they walked.

"For dinner...not yet," she replied and looked up at him, admiring the side of his handsome face with a trace of beard starting to show.

"A drink, then? My turn to buy," he suggested. She stopped walking. He turned to see what was wrong. Moving closer, she raised her hand to his chin and pulled it towards her. Her heart thumped with a delicious anxiety, each beat pushing caution further from her mind.

"In a minute," she whispered. He let his head tilt downward until their noses nearly touched. She moved first, sought and found his lips with hers. They felt warm and soft. He responded to her kiss gently at first, then more urgently--as if to say 'what took you so long'. Her arms went around his neck, and all her doubts evaporated.

She wanted him, surely and completely.

He pulled her close with both arms, his hands moving from the small of her back up to her shoulder blades and back again, as if trying to memorize the curves of her body. Their lips could not get enough of one another. Their tongues met and began a seductive dance, seeking to quench the thirst they each had yet knew it was impossible. Pressed against him, she felt his burgeoning erection through his jeans. He pulled away from her.

"How much further is that hotel?' he asked, his voice rough. She kissed him again. She'd been right--highly kissable lips.

"Not far."

"Good," he said and took hold of both her hands, raised them to his lips and kissed them. "Lead the way." They ran hand in hand the last half block to the Aragon. Almost dark now, they ducked in through the pub entrance to find that Happy Hour had begun and the room crowded with patrons. As they made their way through the tables toward the small lobby, they heard a familiar voice.

"Yoo hoo, over here!" Bette's loud voice called to them from a corner table. They froze like deer in headlights and looked at each other, then over to where Bette and Diggy stood.

"We've hit a check-stop," Zara said.

"Looks that way," Dave agreed. "What do you want to do?"

"Uh, beam us up, Scotty?"

Dave laughed. "As convenient as that would be, don't think that's happening. We'd better go talk to them."

"Briefly," Zara emphasized.

"I do owe you a drink," he said. "Might as well be now-- we might be a little busy later." He squeezed her hand.

"Yeah, that could be," she affirmed. With a smile and a wave, the two of them joined the Ridley's table.

"Well now, what have you two been up to since we last saw you?" asked Bette. Diggy stood, pulling out a chair for Zara and nodding to Dave in greeting.

"Uh, window shopping," Zara said, unable to think of a

better explanation. Realizing they'd not been introduced she added, "Bette and Digbert Ridley, this is David Parker."

"Hello, luv!" Bette said brightly.

"Pleasure," echoed Diggy, shaking Dave's hand, "Call me Diggy."

"I apologize for taking your girl away for the afternoon," Dave said.

"No apologies required, dear boy," Diggy replied, motioning for them both to sit.

"If it were me, I'd be escaping with you and all," Bette said. "And how do you know each other, then; our Zara didn't just pick you up in the Mucky Duck, now did she?"

Dave and Zara exchanged looks. "No, Dave is, ah..." Zara began, not sure how to describe their relationship.

"Actually, she's my boss," Dave said. "I work for Flynn Enterprises. Since Miss Flynn took over as CEO that makes her the head honcho." The Ridleys looked impressed.

"That makes a change eh, woman on top?" Bette quipped.

Wincing, Zara looked over at Dave who without missing a beat said, "I certainly hope so."

Diggy guffawed and raised his pint to Dave in a salute before taking a long swig. Finally, someone had beaten his wife to the punch line.

"Can I buy you folks another drink, Mrs. Ridley?" Dave said, changing the subject before she could react.

Bette paused, looking him over. "Cheeky devil," she said. "Go on, then."

Dave waved to the server. "What can I get you," he asked, pointing to their empty pint glasses.

"I recommend the house dark ale," Diggy said, nodding.

Dave smiled. "House dark, it is." He ordered four.

Elbows on the table, Bette cradled her chin atop interlaced fingers and stared Dave down. "So what do you do then, for a living that is," she said. It sounded more like a command than a question.

"I'm a construction supervisor," he said. "I oversee building projects--handle labour and materials."

Bette raised her chin. "I see. Pays well, does it?"

"Well enough," he said, maintaining eye contact.

Their exchange reminded Zara of a job interview. Bette grilled Dave on his work, his clothes, his eating habits. He took her investigation in stride and seemed to enjoy her attention, but enjoyed outwitting her even more. He adroitly dodged her questions about former girlfriends.

Girlfriends? Zara most definitely didn't want to picture this man with anyone else. The idea made her...good grief... *jealous?* Then she felt Dave's hand touch her knee beneath the table.

Warm fingers roved the surface of her kneecap then traced circles on the inside of her thigh. *Damn, he would drive her crazy if he didn't stop--and she didn't want him to stop.*

CHAPTER EIGHTEEN

The cell phone whirred its soft text signal. Bernardo stood in front of the mirror tying his necktie. He went to check the message. 'Michelle.' Bernardo punched the button, anxious to receive confirmation of his evening. '*lo siento ángel, change of plans, meet saturday instead?*'

Bernardo sat on the edge of the bed. He'd been looking forward to tonight, but what could he say? Something important must have come up. He texted back, '*disappointed but promise saturday, k?*' and waited. The phone vibrated in his hand with a reply. '*k ur mi ángel oscuro, wil txt time Sat.*' Bernardo pressed the return key and set the phone down.

He felt empty now; deflated--despite the use of his secret name, Dark Angel. He decided to go down to the bar, get some dinner and a scotch. And with some unexpected free time on his hands, he might as well catch up on the doings of Miss Flynn.

He chuckled to himself at how easily he'd followed her all day Tuesday, snapping photos at will. Had Verrera enjoyed his artsy nude portrait of her, he wondered? He included it on the USB stick as a bit of a joke, to keep Verrera on his toes.

He sat in the terrace bar, ordered some tapas and polished

off a second scotch. He surveyed the bar carefully, but no sign of Flynn or her English cohorts. Hadn't seen them in the dining room either. Perhaps they'd chosen another restaurant tonight. In any case, he appeared to have plenty of time to wait.

He watched some sports coverage on the TV screens in the bar. He observed guests come and go, on the lookout for his prey. He ordered more scotch. At 8 o'clock he left the bar to have a more thorough look around the Club. He went to the café and back through the dining room, winding up in the lobby. He took note of the desk clerk staff; a fat middle-aged man and a thin woman with eyeglasses suspended on a chain around her neck.

Offhand he wondered where one of the more noticeable clerks, the girl with the big breasts, was tonight. He wandered out to the entrance, moving away from the doors and the well-lit steps toward the shrubbery hidden in shadows. He stopped to have a good look around. The fragrance of flowering bushes hung heavily in the cool night air.

A few guests were moving about but no trace of Flynn or the others. Frustrated, he decided to take a more direct approach. Picking up some hotel literature and a local paper on his way through the lobby, he rang for the elevator and got in. Stepping onto the tenth floor he made his way to 1004. A general sweep of the area revealed nothing. Behind its' closed door, no obvious sounds came from inside the suite. Miss Flynn appeared to be out.

A settee and a console table situated near the elevators provided a good vantage point. He made himself comfortable and pulled out his newspapers and brochures. Putting on a pair of reading glasses, he made his best effort to look like a nondescript hotel guest.

He noted the big green marble urn set between the elevator doors. The same on every floor, they made a suitable receptacle for his cardkey a few nights ago--for the convenience of his mystery guest. Wishing he could be entertaining that guest right now instead of posting a stake-out, he sighed and pretended to read his brochures. And waited.

At 8:45 he heard someone coming. He kept his head down and watched from behind his papers. The big-chested desk clerk walked up to the elevators, obviously off-shift as she'd dressed in regular street clothes. She pushed the button for the elevator and as Bernardo watched, slipped a cardkey into the green urn. In a few moments she disappeared into the elevator.

Waiting for the closing thud of the doors, Bernardo's mind began to race. Who else knew about this trick? *It could just be coincidence.* It would be a likely place to hide a key. No one but the owner would know which door it opened, unless they tried every door in the hotel. A light switched on in Bernardo's mind and on a hunch, fished the cardkey out of the urn.

Making certain no one watched, he approached the door to 1004 and swiped the card in the lock. Miraculously, the green light went on and he pushed the lever without making a sound. He placed his newspaper in the door jamb and listened for any movement from inside the room. Nothing. He returned the cardkey to the urn and crept inside the suite. He didn't turn on any lights as he ventured deeper into the room.

As his eyes adjusted to the dimness, the room appeared unused since housekeeping had been there. Everything seemed in place, beds made, towels changed and folded. He didn't see any luggage lying around. He smelled the fragrance of flowers from a vase on the coffee table and noted an ice bucket with champagne and glasses set out as if company were expected. Interesting, he thought. It might be very helpful to know whom Miss Flynn planned to entertain.

Bernardo went toward the faint light coming from the windows. Unlatching the shutters, he stepped out onto the balcony. Out of plain view of the other rooms, he felt it safe to wait there. He closed the shutters and adjusted the vanes to allow for sight and sound from inside the room. He settled himself on a patio chair in a corner of the balcony and pressed a button on his watch to illuminate the face. 8:55.

He inhaled the night air, taking a rare moment to appreciate the fragrance of the surrounding flowers and the faint sounds of faraway traffic. The moment didn't last long however, as some action stirred within the room. He heard the door open and soft footsteps come into the main area. A switch tripped on and the strip lighting around the bedroom area began to glow. A vague silhouette moved about and he heard the rattle of ice cubes in the champagne bucket. The sound of a struck match and the glow of candles being lit.

The figure moved slowly around the room, arranging things as if preparing for a royal visit. He heard a zipper opening and as he peered through the shutter vanes, made out the shape of a woman. She removed clothing from a carry bag and began to change. He looked away, scanned the area outside the balcony, checking for other spectators. Too many floors up for people on the ground to see and no visible guests on nearby balconies.

The woman put some music on. The slow exotic sounds of Indian music, with plenty of sitar and finger cymbals, began to play. She swayed to the music as if performing for a private audience. Bernardo checked his watch again. 9:25pm. She stopped dancing and began to pace back and forth.

It appeared her guest was running late.

The figure came toward the balcony doors. Bernardo shrank back into his corner. She pushed the shutters open and stepped out onto the dark balcony. She leaned on the railing with her back to him, looking out into the night as if she could wish upon a star for her visitor to arrive.

Bernardo hadn't come to 1004 for this purpose, but the opportunity to eliminate one of his obstacles materialized right in front of him. With the alternative being discovered spying on her, the decision was easy. He lunged three steps toward her, full force. She began to turn just as he hit her, his elbow and shoulder smashing into her side and toppling her over the railing.

As she fell he could see the gauzy material of her outfit flailing about her and realized with horror, it wasn't Zara Flynn.

As if in slow motion, the busty desk clerk landed on the ground ten stories below him. He backed up from the railing, groping for the shutters and clambering back into the hotel room. What was she doing in 1004 and where was Flynn? Panicking, he took a moment to gather his wits but it cost him.

The door lock clicked open as someone swiped a cardkey in the reader outside. Whirling to face the door, he froze in place as he a saw a man in a dark suit hold open the door for someone to enter. There, framed in the light from the hallway, stood Michelle.

Bernardo gaped, realizing with agony that Michelle wasn't Michelle tonight. She'd exchanged her costume for her true self.

Miguel paused in the doorway staring at Bernardo. Speechless for a moment, he motioned for Luis to follow him in and close the door.

"¿Que haces aqui?" Miguel said, with quiet accusation in his voice. "Why are you here," he repeated more sharply, in English.

"¿Y usted? I could ask the same question," Bernardo replied. "This was your change of plans? Chasing the skirt of the puta Canadiense?" Jealousy rose inside him.

"That's none of your business, Ángel. Answer me, que has echo? Donde está la Señoritá Flynn?" Miguel glared at him, stone-faced. The look sent a stab of anguish through Bernardo. How dare he question his choices? With this he'd damaged his relationship with Michelle/Miguel beyond repair, and terror grew in the pit of his stomach over the body lying in the bushes below.

"See for yourself," Bernardo hissed. He found the will to move aside, gesturing to the open balcony doors. Miguel signalled Luis to check them, keeping one eye on Cruz. Only candlelight flickered in the room and when Miguel looked away, Bernardo bolted for the door.

CHAPTER NINETEEN

The first beams of sunrise cut across the bed from the not-quite-closed curtains. A slight wind waffled them as it blew through the open window and the calls of seabirds could be heard in the distance. David lay wide awake, feeling the breeze on his skin, listening to the birds, taking in every detail of the moment. The white paneled walls, the cool cotton of the sheets and most of all, the gorgeous girl sleeping next to him.

He wanted to touch her, kiss her, make love to her again as he had last night and hear her soft moans as he pleasured her. But he didn't dare to wake her just yet. The picture was so perfect, so blissful, he felt suspended in time and feared that if he moved a muscle the scene might burst like a bubble and be only a dream.

He breathed deeply to catch the scent of her perfume. He tried to commit to memory the look of her hair cascading across the pillow, her eyelashes, the lightly freckled nose, the silver chain and dolphin pendant nestled at her collarbone.

The white sheet partially covered her nude body. One hand rested across her stomach, the other palm-up on the pillow. One breast lay exposed and risking that the dream could shatter, he leaned down and licked the nipple, feeling the bumpy texture of it against his tongue. Christ, he felt hard again already. He loved everything about this woman, wanted to possess her forever.

He moved upward with his tongue, tracing a line to her throat, over her chin and across her lips. Her closed eyes began to twitch and flutter open. She blinked, bringing him into focus. A smile crept across her face as she looked back at him. He almost felt relieved that she recognized him--that it hadn't all been a dream and she was here in the present with him. He smiled down at her. "Good morning, Montreal."

"Hey, Thunder Bay," she replied. "Or should I say, Thunder Boy?" She grinned sleepily. Dave hoped he hadn't made quite as much noise during their lovemaking as all that; but if he'd made her feel like she'd been caught in a crashing, rollicking Great Lakes thunderstorm--and liked it--that pleased him. She reached up and put her hand on his cheek. "Are you real?" He turned his face so that her finger slipped between his lips and he bit it gently.

"Afraid so, mademoiselle. Anything else you'd like to know?"

She smiled mischievously. "Yeah, are you ready for round two?"

He raised his eyebrows twice in a villainous fashion and leaned down to kiss her. "Ding, ding," he answered, mimicking a ringside bell. He let their lips find each other again as he pulled the sheet away. He lay against her, his stiff cock showing her exactly how ready he was.

His hand followed the outer curve of her breast with an open palm then circled the edge of her nipple with his fingertips. They stiffened instantly and he could hear her soft sigh even though he kept her lips fully occupied. He broke their kiss in favour of taking the taut, pink-brown berry in his mouth. He swirled his tongue around it and sucked, thinking no food or drink on earth would ever taste this sweet. She groaned and leaned her head back against the pillow. *Oh, he could do so much more for her*.

Taking more of her breast in his mouth he sucked harder and slid his hand down to her hip, then across her abdomen. Settling his fingers in her pubic hair, he rubbed her mound gently before sliding a finger into the wetness between her legs. She gasped and arched her back as she moved into his touch. Her slickness made his dick throb with wanting to enter her. But not yet.

He stroked her sweet hot-button of flesh and heard her breath catch with each pass. He slipped one finger inside her, then two, moving them slowly in and out until she moaned aloud.

The pressure of blood in his dick rose to a maddening level. He felt as though he'd break apart if he didn't fuck her right this second--but no, he'd finish her and watch it happen. His mouth left her breasts and he dragged his lips across and down her belly. He heard his own voice whispering her name, "Zara..." though it sounded ethereal and bodiless as if floating above them.

Instinctively she raised her knees and Dave thought he just might die of pleasure as he brought his head between her thighs and tasted her sex, his tongue taking plunging strokes against her clit.

Her hands rested on his head, fingers entwined in his hair as she followed his motion. He looked up and incredibly, saw her gazing directly back at him as he continued his magic. Their eyes locked while he worked his clever tongue against her until he pushed her over the edge, watching her as she came. He could taste it, smell it; knew he'd reached his goal of bringing her to orgasm.

Her eyelids closed as if overwhelmed by the power of it. Her hands trembled as they remained tangled in his hair. Now. He needed her now and moved his body overtop her.

She wrapped her arms around his neck and drew her thighs up on either side of him. So hot and wet, he slid easily into her and felt like he'd been granted permission to enter heaven itself.

Joy and lust collided in his soul as he drove deep, without restraint, again and again. She kissed his face, his neck, rubbed her hands up and down the muscles of his back as she moved in sync with each thrust, accepting him deeply and completely.

She held him tight as he climaxed. *Sweet mother of God.* He felt as if caught in an avalanche, tumbling helpless and unthinking in a white storm of sexual release. His mind blanked, aware of nothing but the hammering of his heart in his chest and the hot fluid pumping from him into her. He took in deep, ragged breaths as his heartbeat slowed, recovering. He nuzzled her neck and when he raised his head, saw tears in her eyes.

"Oh, God, I'm sorry," he said in a strained voice. "Have I hurt you, please, tell me…" She reached up to touch his lips, as if to stop the words from coming out.

"Much worse," she said. "You've made me fall in love with you."

He looked into her watery eyes, seeing the truth there. He kissed her fingertips, knowing it was fast, crazy and wonderful all at the same time. Just because it happened fast, didn't mean it wasn't right.

"Oh dear," he said in a regretful tone. "There's only one cure for that." He stroked the sandy blond hair falling across her forehead and wiped away the tears from the beautiful green eyes with his thumb. "And that's to love you right back."

*

When he'd finished in the shower, Dave returned to the main room to see Zara sitting in a chair facing the mirror.

Wrapped in the fluffy hotel bathrobe, she held her cell phone to her ear. He supposed they had to check out soon, but honestly hadn't thought about the time for the last several hours. Several incredible hours.

He'd lost count how many times they'd made love. He hadn't used any protection; but she hadn't asked for any, either. It wasn't like him to be careless in that regard. Well, maybe once or twice. It seemed they'd both lost their heads a bit. Or perhaps found them. A deep and wordless understanding seemed to exist between them, one that foreshadowed the future. Then it dawned on him how much he wanted that future.

He approached her from behind, placing his hands on her shoulders then slipping them down under her arms and around her waist. He rested his chin on her shoulder and gazed at their faces framed in the mirror. Still naked, his reflection showed off muscular arms and tanned shoulders as he held her fast in the chair. He hadn't any shaving tools with him, so he sported a Marlboro-Man stubble as he smiled his brilliant, dimpled smile at her. He hoped she liked the rugged look. The line picked up.

"Jorge," said Zara. Buenas días."

"Buenas Días, Miss. I am en route now. Esta problema?"

"No hay problema," she replied. "Just wanted to ask, would you mind driving the Ridleys back to the Club? I'm going to drive back separately, stop in at El Mirador."

"Certainly Miss, but what are you driving? Have you rented a car?"

"Well, Jorge, I ran into Mr. Parker here in Gib and we're going to drive back together in the company truck."

Dave heard Jorge's words coming over her handset and listened with curious amusement to her answers. He squeezed her tight, pretending to pant and lick her face like a rambunctious puppy. She tried not to giggle into the phone and fended him off while she concentrated on her conversation.

"Muy bien, Miss. I will be at the Aragon about noon. Have a safe trip back."

"Gracias Jorge, I'll meet you at the entrance to say goodbye, adios!" She disconnected the call and tossed the cell phone on the dresser. Trapped in the chair, she reached up and grabbed Dave by his hair with both hands. "Okay Thunder Boy, that's enough!"

"Ouch." He released her from his grip. Zara rose from the chair and wagged her forefinger at him.

"Be a good dog, now." She stepped towards him, letting the bathrobe slip to the floor. He embraced her and revelled in the sensation of their bodies touching from head to toe.

"We'd better get moving," he said softly. "Or I'll need another shower, a cold one." As she relaxed against him, he found himself wondering how he could have ever felt truly alive before today. Reluctantly, he let go as she went into the bathroom to put on her makeup and pack her things. When she'd closed the door, he laid down on his stomach on the unmade bed, propping his head on his elbows.

They hadn't slept much, but he'd never felt more energized than he did right now. This changed things, his relationship with Zara. Could this work, with them both at the same job, or worse, could it work if she decided not to stay? His plans for moving up in the company might take a sharp turn either way.

Would she feel betrayed if he told her why Tristan had been on the Indonesian job? The question stabbed at his heart like a knife and set the man's words echoing in his ears. *"Get yourself back here. We need your young blood, Youngblood. I'll not have you dying of some poxy jungle fever."*

If Dave hadn't come back he'd never have met her. But if Tristan had returned...same result. Sometimes the truth sucked. They were so right for each other and had so much in common. Not only their work and where they'd come from but also a deep loyalty to one person. It was too much coincidence for them to meet here, now, for it not to be fate. *It has to work out*, he decided. *It must work out.*

Right now it felt like he'd die if it didn't.

CHAPTER TWENTY

Zara and Dave walked into the lobby, where Bette and Diggy stood waiting at the checkout desk. Bette spotted them first. "Aww, there you are, you two. It's almost noon, don't tell me you were canoodling right up 'til now?"

Bette had a way of telling it straight. You were never left doubting what she meant about anything. It's what Zara liked about her most. And it wasn't really a secret what she and Dave had been up to. It had been pretty obvious in the bar last night what was going on between them.

"Well," Zara said, "the Guinness people were unavailable for comment, but I think we may have broken some sort of record."

Bette laughed and patted Diggy on the shoulder saying, "Let's get a move on, Dig."

"Jorge will be here in a few minutes," Zara said. I hope you don't mind if I send you back to Marbella with him? Dave and I are going to make a stop along the way." Bette eyed her dubiously.

"Really, business stuff," Zara reassured her.

"Of course, dearie," Bette said, rolling her eyes. "Two young lovebirds are always stopping to…take care of business." Then she turned to Dave, pointing a pink-painted finger at him. "You bring our girl back safe, yeah? I'll never forgive you if you don't."

"Leave the lad alone, luv," Diggy said as he joined them. "I'm sure he's the responsible type, aren't you, mate?" He reached out for a handshake.

Dave returned the handshake and nodded. "I can tell you with complete confidence, Mr. & Mrs. Ridley, she'll be in good hands."

Diggy laughed aloud, shaking his head. "Young lady, this lad's a right scream. You hang on to this one. He'll have you laughing 'til your golden years."

Dave really did have quite a sense of humour. Zara wished she could have appreciated it more on the day they first met. If only she hadn't been so hung over.

"Thank you dear, for a lovely trip," Bette said, taking Zara's hands in hers. "You take care and we'll see you back at the Club, right?"

"You're welcome, Bette. Thanks for being so understanding." Zara hugged her and the four of them strolled out to the street to meet Jorge.

*

Ignacio pulled the car up on his cobblestone drive. As he got out of the driver's side, the front door of the house burst open. Daniela and Ericka came running out. Their Aunt Maria followed in their wake, stopping in the doorway. She'd brought the girls back to the house to greet their mother home from hospital.

"Mami," they called, jumping up and down with excitement. Ignacio helped Carmella out of the car and her girls swarmed to her, putting their arms around her. Carmella smiled and hugged them both.

"Be careful, girls," their dad said. "Mama is still very tired from the hospital, take it easy." He looked at his sister Maria as she hung back on the doorstep. "Gracias, Maria. I can't thank you enough for staying with them."

Ignacio guided his wife into the house then returned to collect the rest of her things from the car. Maria spoke.

"You know she's very lucky, Ignacio. Many people don't live through a heart attack. I hope this is a wake-up call for you both." Ignacio put his arm around her shoulder.

"Maria, I think things are going to be very different from now on."

*

Miguel sat on a deck chair on the penthouse balcony staring out to the sea. He tried to compose himself after last night's incident. He had a performance to prepare for. The show must go on.

Delores had broken her neck in the fall off the tenth floor balcony. Not one, but two of his lovers had been compromised in this affair and it pained his soul that anyone had been hurt. His world was about love, not revenge or jealousy.

'Michelle' had been but one of many alter egos he assumed while pursuing his less conventional affairs. In a way, he was like Delores in that he enjoyed 'dressing up,' too. It turned him on, to pretend to be female--just as much as females turned him on as a man.

Sadly Bernardo, his 'dark angel' could no longer be part of the entourage. Miguel could not tolerate such an act of aggression. He didn't know where Cruz had run to. He'd sent Raoul to track him down, but Cruz managed to slip away. Luis and Miguel saw to the discovery of Delores' body by hotel security, without directly revealing themselves. He hoped they'd find her still alive, but they were too late.

Miguel tried to piece together how and why this happened. Why was Bernardo on the 10th floor with Delores in the room?

Why would he have killed her? Where was Miss Flynn? Had Bernardo found out about Delores' relationship with the singing star and killed her out of jealousy?

Miguel remembered Cruz' words. 'La puta Canadiense', the Canadian whore. Was it Miss Flynn he was really after? Perhaps he expected to find her in 1004 just as Miguel had. Poor Delores, she'd wanted to be with Miguel so badly she unknowingly put herself in harm's way.

Delores always made the room arrangements--she could easily have moved Flynn elsewhere and lain in wait for him in her place. A disquiet gathered over him like gray storm clouds. He needed to find Cruz before he harmed his intended target. That meant he had to find Zara.

*

Bernardo ran blindly out of suite 1004 not really sure where to go. He just felt lucky to escape. Knowing Montana's delicate situation, he wouldn't have alerted hotel security or the police. This bought him enough time to find a hiding place.

Cramped in the trunk of his car in the hotel parkade, he'd been here several hours now, thinking and listening. But his bodily functions couldn't be denied much longer.

He felt frightened and desperate. Not only had he failed to take Miss Flynn out of the picture, he'd killed an innocent woman. Worse still, he'd lost Michelle. This one result made him weep more than either of the others. He wouldn't have that joy ever again and his despair soon gave way to anger. Flynn was in the way. He needed to proceed with the next phase of the plan. He could wait a little longer, until dusk fell. Then he would make his move.

CHAPTER TWENTY-ONE

Zara converted the straps of her red patent bag to backpack position. She loved its versatility, large enough to serve as everything from handbag to briefcase to shopping bag. She donned her one change of clothes, a pair of beige cotton capris and a white tank top.

Her hair seemed to have acclimated itself and she'd given up doing anything but letting it flow loose and free. Dave didn't seem to mind. They'd missed the complimentary breakfast, so they stopped at an outdoor market to fill the red bag with food and drinks for the road.

As they drove east, El Mirador appeared in the distance. Zara talked about what she'd found on the internet and how none if it revealed the complete story behind its current condition. The closer they came to it, the more anxious Zara felt. So agitated by the time they drew within a kilometre or so, she asked Dave to pull over and take a walk.

The mid-afternoon sun scorched the beach. They found a path from the lookout point that led down to the sea. The shimmering white sand spread before them in both directions and they set out barefoot for the water's edge. The waves lapped at their toes as they walked hand in hand. It felt so good.

"You're awfully quiet," Dave said. "What's on your mind?"

Zara tried to sort out her emotions before answering. "It's hard to explain. There just doesn't seem to be a reason for my Dad to leave El Mirador to me. I can't figure it out. Restoring it would cost millions. Tearing it down feels like there's no point in having it in the first place. I feel nervous, now. Like I shouldn't be here."

"Yes, you should," Dave said. "Otherwise I wouldn't have met you." They walked a few more steps in silence, then he stopped and turned her to face him. "Everything happens for a reason. You're here. I'm here. We're together for a reason, I'm sure of it. So is El Mirador. The reason will come, don't think about it so hard."

She tried to do as he asked and clear her mind. Placing one foot in front of the other, she concentrated on the feel of the sand between her toes and the warmth of his hand in hers as they walked on.

"Why did Ernesto ask you about explosives?" she finally said.

Dave looked out over the water for a long minute. He chewed his lower lip as if trying out potential answers in his mind before speaking. "He's worried about a potential saboteur."

"What? Why?"

"Because of what happened in Java."

She slowed her pace and regarded him suspiciously. The words came rushing back to her. *Sabotage. Explosive demolition. Short-staffed. Overtime.*

"So it wasn't an accident. You're telling me for certain that my father died in a deliberate act of destruction," she said, her voice monotone.

Dave took a deep breath in. "We think so, yes."

She wanted to verify what she'd read, see if his answer would corroborate the story. "Ernesto said he went there sooner than he'd planned. Do you know why?"

He hesitated and kept looking straight ahead. "Because I left."

Zara stopped in her tracks. "What do you mean? You were there?" Her mouth dropped open in disbelief. "And you never said anything…"

He pulled her by the hand to face him. "Hold on, I wasn't with him. Yes, I did go there, Tristan asked me if I wanted the foreman's' job. We were short of trained workers. I went to check it out and I got sick. They had to fly me back inside of a week. That's when he decided to go there himself."

She felt dizzy. *Dad left. Dave came back.* She didn't like where this thought was going. *I wasn't allowed to have both men. One or the other would have died there. Could fate be that cruel?* Her balance began to waver and Dave took her in his arms to keep her from falling.

"Hey, you know what," he said, verbally shifting gears. "We haven't eaten anything since yesterday. Let's take a break, crack open that wine. Maybe you'll feel better."

They'd been walking towards El Mirador all this time. It stood only a few hundred metres ahead. "Yeah, okay," she said in surrender, tired of thinking. "But I've got another idea." The surrounding beach lay studded with rocks and sharp outcroppings. Not much for shade, they found a spot between several boulders that afforded not only protection from the sun, but privacy as well.

Zara put down her bag, which held the bottle of wine and a selection of cheeses, olives and fruit bought at the market in Gibraltar. She surprised Dave when she began to take off her clothes.

"I'm going for a swim," she announced. "How about you?"

"Hell of an idea," Dave said and quickly doffed his shirt

and jeans. Naked, they both ran for the water and dove in. Zara felt completely free, as if the water could wash away all her concerns. She swam underwater for a few strokes, then surfaced, flipping onto her back and just floating.

The water and the sun caressed their bodies, entreating them to let go of troublesome thoughts and just exist in the moment. They swam alongside one another then embraced and kissed, weightless in the water.

They made their way back to the boulders, opened the wine and munched on fruit, cheese and olives. They didn't bother getting dressed.

"Well, this has to be the first nude picnic I've ever been to," Dave said. "We really must do this more often. Invite the neighbours, y'know?" More relaxed now, Zara laughed. *Diggy was right,* she thought. He would keep her laughing until they were old and gray.

She felt a sudden surge of bittersweet emotion. She'd fallen in love with him, no help for that, now. But what he'd said about her father taking his place struck so deep a chord of irony within her, it made her chest ache. She looked across the short distance between them, her mind a mass of mixed feelings.

He had a great body. Clearly he worked out. A smooth, well-muscled chest and flat stomach. Legs that looked like he spent some time running. And she'd been with enough men to know he'd been…gifted…in the size of his penis. In spite of the heat, she shivered with the memory of their lovemaking that was both wildly sensual and tender beyond words.

I must be crazy…I barely know this guy…we work together, this can't end well. Yet I know we belong together.

Left to dry in the sun, his hair had quite a bit of wave in it. The ends curled up around his face. She set down her wine and went to him, a sense of purpose becoming clear to her as she drew near.

He lay on his back, on top of his t-shirt and jeans with his arms behind his head, gazing up at the sky. He looked like a modern-day Tarzan. She knelt down beside him and catching him off-guard, swung her leg over and straddled him like a horse. She sat upright, looking down on him.

"Whoa now," he managed to say. "Uh, let me guess. Girls in Barrie are sent to equestrian school for summer camp?"

For a change she got the last words in. "No. I went to… *private* school," she said, winking. "You've got your wish, Thunder Boy. Woman on top."

He looked up at her and fell silent. He reached up and cupped her breasts in both hands, brushing the nipples with his thumbs. She felt the sweetly painful tingle as they hardened and stood erect at his touch. She closed her eyes and let him explore as he wished. Then she leaned forward to kiss him. He moved his hands up to her face, stopping her a few inches away.

Looking into her eyes, he mouthed the words, "I love you," then brought her lips to his.

Her heart clenched and Zara emptied all the passion she felt into this one kiss. She yearned to pleasure him in ways no one else could. She wanted to forget everything but this moment. If she was allowed only one man, then she would have every square inch, every last drop of this one.

She tasted the salt on his lips, explored his mouth with her tongue. She could feel his heartbeat accelerating, his breath rapid. *Good, good…come with me, let me lead where no one else can take you.*

His dick grew hard against her inner thigh as she lay atop him, her legs hugging his hips. She kissed his neck, his Adam's apple, worked her way across his chest, flicking her tongue against his tight, contoured pecs.

He groaned. And she smiled.

Just you wait, Thunder Boy…show's not nearly over.

She wriggled lower, tickling him mercilessly by brushing her lips against his hard stomach. Something about the area of his body just around his navel made her ultra-aroused. She felt her own sexual muscles contract in anticipation...*when did I become this naughty,* she wondered, amazed she could think at all.

She reached to take his erection in her hands, her touch as deft as with clay on a potters' wheel. Stroking it, she rubbed the tip with her thumbs, the preliminary warm fluid presenting itself there. She felt his hands on her shoulders, his fingertips digging into her skin.

She licked the stray fluid from the tip, heard his breath hitch and another groan escape his lips. She swallowed the starchy liquid that tasted faintly like fresh bread. Her mouth closed around the satiny head of his dick, tasting him as thoroughly as he'd tasted her.

She heard a whispered "oh, babe..." as she held the tip against the roof of her mouth and sucked with a pulsating rhythm. She took all of him in, bore down on him until the head bumped the back of her throat.

He groaned helplessly.

Zara eased off, withdrawing him from her mouth like a popsicle on a hot summer day. She sat up, grinning at the power she wielded over him. She heard far-off calls of birds and smelled the pungent, late afternoon air as it found its way to them in spite of the sheltering rock.

His eyes snapped open as the sudden wisp of breeze touched his wet member. He made quite a sight, fully aroused and the question of 'what next' written across his face.

Her grin turned devilish as she rose up on her knees and placed herself upon him, fitting him into her with a calculated slowness. *Oh, God yes, he felt so good inside her.*

Her next moves took even her by surprise. She rode him like a saddle bronc, satisfying some base, primal need that she didn't realize she possessed until this moment. Her hips rose and fell at a pace and force she alone decided, taking control of her own pleasure, filling herself with him to the max.

Dave caught her by her wrists as she flipped her head back and two final grinding pushes sent him past his breaking point. Her warm body encased him, felt his muscle pulsing as she coaxed every drop of seed from him.

His eyes clenched shut and he laughed softly as he surrendered to her. When it subsided, she held him close, bestowing soft butterfly kisses on his face, his neck and the tops of his ears.

He belonged to her now. She'd left a mark on him as telling as a scar.

"You are," he said, stroking her hair, "…an absolute Goddess. What you do to me…I'm speechless."

Zara giggled. *Mr. Smart-Ass? Speechless?* "It's about time," she said.

"You realize payback will be significant."

"I consider it an investment," she said, laying her head against the moist skin of his chest, her hand exploring its muscular landscape.

For a long while they lay entwined together in the sand, serenaded by the hushed sounds of waves cresting and retreating while the sun sank low in the sky.

"If you still want to have a look around El Mirador, we'd better do it now," Dave said. She agreed and they began to dress, brushing sand from themselves and their belongings as they prepared to leave.

"It's only a few hundred metres," Zara said. "Let's just walk."

"You sure?" he asked. Zara nodded. They'd come this far and her earlier foreboding had dissipated. They walked along the beach, seeing the ragged outline of El Mirador loom larger with every step.

*

Bernardo made it out of the parkade without notice. He drove fast along the highway, the setting sun glaring in the windshield as he went west. He slowed at the exit to El Mirador, parking at the same lookout point as before.

Carefully, he took the laptop case from behind the driver's seat and walked down the embankment, out of sight from the road. He sat on a flat rock and peered through binoculars to ensure no potential witnesses were in sight. He scanned the beach, the surrounding area and even out to sea, checking for boaters. Nothing.

He took out the detonator device from the laptop case then visually swept the beach one more time. Something caught his eye.

Of all things, two people walked on the beach on a direct course for the scarecrowish remains of El Mirador. His binoculars zoomed in on them. Adjusting the focus, Cruz could make out a man and a woman dressed in casual clothing, seemingly doing nothing more than taking a stroll on the beach. He zoomed in to maximum and let out a stifled grunt upon realizing what he saw.

Flynn, and what looked like one of the men from Wednesday's site visit, walked directly toward the abandoned structure. Looking around, touching the pillars, pointing and talking to each other. He blinked, recalling he'd actually seen this man before.

At the airport in Jakarta.

Bernardo closed his eyes. He'd waited this long; he could wait a little longer until they progressed so far into the building they wouldn't escape in time. He trained his binoculars on them, held the device close to his chest and waited for the right moment.

*

She noticed the smell first. The pigeons cooed and clucked, shifting around their perches and flying about as she and Dave approached the elevator column. Despite their presence, it occurred to Zara what had bothered her about the previous visit.

"Can't you smell it?" she asked. Dave stood still, listened and inhaled. A melange of many odours wafted around them, not the least of which was pigeon dung. He shook his head, unsure which smell she referred to. They stood at the opening to the elevator well. A good twenty-foot drop stretched down to the basement, as they knew.

"It's oil, crude oil," she said in a quiet voice, prompting him for recognition. "Think, haven't you smelled that before, in a garage or automotive shop? Greasy lube stuff, like when you get an oil change?" He looked at her and nodded. Zara gazed down the black shaft of the concrete well. "There's one way to find out for sure," she said.

"Oh, you're not going down there, no way. We're not supposed to be here, Ernie would freak if he knew I'd brought you back here, this close. We don't have safety gear and it's twenty feet down, for God's sake. What was I thinking…I'm such an idiot." He grabbed her arm to pull her away and get them both the hell out of there.

They started to move away when Zara stopped short. She looked down at her feet, then up at Dave. The color drained from her face.

"What?" Dave asked, grabbing her by both arms. "C'mon babe, we gotta go, it's getting dark," he urged. A panicky shudder coursed up her spine, as though she'd stuck her finger in a light socket. She felt rooted to the spot, vibrating. It lasted a split-second, then her eyes went wide as she looked at Dave and choked out one word.

"...Run...!"

He bolted, half dragging, half lifting her along with him. The sound deafened them and the ground shook beneath their feet. Dust filled the air and she couldn't see him, only feel her arm in his grip. Chunks of concrete rained down like mammoth hailstones and she felt the ground give way. Dave grabbed hold of her around her waist and dropped into a roll, hurling them outward from the building. It was the last thing she remembered.

*

Cruz sat pinned to the rock, the device in his hand. The building hadn't come completely down. Perhaps he didn't plant the charges in exactly in the right spots. But he'd done enough damage to end anyone's plans of restoring the structure. He waited for the dust to clear, watching through the binoculars for any sign of movement. After about ten minutes, darkness shrouded the deadly scene. He put the detonator back in the laptop case and scrambled back up the bank.

CHAPTER TWENTY-TWO

Maria prepared to leave her brother's house. She'd stayed long enough to help Carmella get settled and cook dinner for the family, but told Ignacio privately that things must change between him and his wife if he wanted his girls to have a mother beyond the next few years.

"Good advice," he told her. "Good things are coming, Maria. Trust me."

While they chatted on the patio, he glanced through the kitchen window and watched Carmella re-organize the cabinets. She disliked strangers in her house. They girls had gone to watch a DVD in the playroom after supper. As she rearranged plates and cutlery, Ignacio wondered what Carmella had thought about in the past 72 hours. Her health, her marriage, her daughters?

He'd stayed nearly three whole days in hospital, not leaving her side. Surely this would mean something to her-- and demonstrate his effort to improve.

Lucky to be alive this time, what would prevent another heart attack from happening to Carmella? His daughters must be provided for, in the event she wasn't so lucky next time. He should meet with a lawyer as soon as possible to review the will. As Carmella took a broom from the closet, Ignacio turned away from the window and walked Maria to her car.

As she swept along the kick plates of the cabinets, something skittered out into the middle of the floor. Carmella bent down to pick it up and blew the dust off it. Examining it for a moment, she slipped it into her pocket and continued sweeping. Maria's car started and backed out of the driveway. Ignacio stepped into the kitchen.

"An excellent dinner, my dear," he said. "We could have ordered out you know, you didn't have to cook. You just got home. How do you feel?" He tried his best to seem concerned and complimentary.

"I feel fine," she said. "But I should probably rest now. Why don't you run the girls their bath and get them ready for bed so I can sit for awhile."

Ignacio nodded. "Of course, dear. You should take things slow; I'll look after them, you relax. Can I make you a coffee before I go?"

"No, the caffeine would be bad for me, you tend to the girls."

"Alright." He decided to change the subject. "Do you remember, I said there were a few projects underway for my new company? Well, I think things will start to happen this week and we could be seeing a profit very soon. I think you will be pleased."

She looked back at him, gave him a vaguely supportive smile. He knew she'd never felt confident about his 'projects.' Even he admitted he'd not been much of a success at anything outside of his day job. But this time…this time he'd show her.

"That's nice, Ignacio. I'm happy for you."

He beamed as though he'd just sunk a difficult putt. "Be happy for *us*," he corrected and gave her a kiss on the cheek on his way to the playroom.

Carmella leaned against the kitchen counter while her

husband and daughters trouped upstairs. Then she went into Ignacio's office. Except to collect coffee cups and occasionally empty the ashtray after Ignacio had indulged in one of his nasty cigars, she seldom went there. She walked to the computer desk and sat down. The screen was dark but the computer's power light glowed green.

She took the memory stick from her pocket and fitted it into one of the ports before switching on the monitor.

*

Ignacio let the girls splash around in the tub while he went to lay out their pyjamas. His good mood made him feel like whistling. He felt certain Bernardo would have news for him soon.

The bid proposals for the El Mirador property had been drawn up for weeks. It would only be a matter of time until they were accepted; the site would be next to worthless after Bernardo finished with it. Nearly ready for tenants, he expected his two downtown projects to start producing a positive cash flow any time. Vistamar was becoming a reality.

He returned to the bathroom and opened the door just wide enough to tell the girls to get out of the tub and dry off. "Go put on your pyjamas and pick out a book; then I'll come read to you."

He went down the hall to his own bedroom and searched in the bottom drawer of his nightstand, withdrawing a plain brown envelope. He just couldn't help taking another look at the papers, to assure himself that all his dreams would soon be real.

He pulled them from the envelope and scanned over them. The proposal lay on top, outlining the 'clean up' plans and offer to purchase for barely ¼ of the market price. The incorporation papers for Vistamar lay beneath that, the name of the principal stakeholder appearing at the bottom.

The shadowy Salvatore Rodriguez.

Ignacio chuckled to himself. Bernardo did brilliant work. No one knew that Vistamar's principal and the regional development officer were the same person.

He shoved the papers back inside. Instead of returning them to the drawer, he decided to keep the documents a little closer at hand. He folded the envelope and stuffed it in his back pocket. He planned to go down to his office as soon as the girls were in bed. He heard them in their bedroom, laughing and arguing over which stuffed toys they would take to bed. He peeked into their room, bade them pick out their storybooks and get under the covers.

"I will be back to read to you in two minutes," he said, holding up two fingers.

"Okay, papa," they said and leaped in unison on top of their twin beds, bouncing up and down. Ignacio shook his head, smiling at their antics. He closed their door and started down the stairs.

The sound of smashing glass startled him and he nearly slipped and fell five steps from the landing. A second, muffled crash came--from inside his office. Confused, he hurried to his office door and flung it open.

There, in front of his cigar humidor stood Carmella, brandishing an old soccer trophy he kept on one of his bookshelves. She'd broken the glass door of the humidor and boxes of his prized collection lay scattered over the floor, smashed and stomped on. His mouth dropped open in horror at the look on his wife's face.

Her eyebrows knitted together over glaring eyes. She didn't speak, but pointed to the computer. He'd forgotten all about what he'd been doing before Carmella had collapsed in the kitchen three days ago. The last picture he'd been viewing displayed on the screen, zoomed in tight. The image of a topless Zara Flynn.

"Vete de aqui!" It sounded more like a growl than a scream. It rose in pitch as she repeated, "Vete de aqui! Get Out!" She advanced toward him, the heavy trophy on its wooden base in her hand. Ignacio backed up, stumbled over the threshold of his office door. "Get out, and don't come back!"

She raised the trophy higher, as if meaning to strike him with it. Ignacio turned and ran. The keys still in his pocket, he dashed madly to his car and backed out of the driveway having no idea where he would go.

*

"Have you found her yet?" Miguel asked, as Luis entered the dressing room.

Luis shook his head. "Nor Cruz, either. His car is not on resort property. Senorita Flynn moved to room 514 three days ago but she is currently out. We are looking for Sr. and Sra. Ridley, the elderly couple she's been seen with during her stay here. Perhaps they'll know something."

Miguel sat in his dressing room chair, elbows on his knees and fingertips pressed together. "Bien, Luis. If you find her, please bring her to me as you did before. She needs to know the danger she is in."

"Is there anything else?" Luis asked as he turned to leave, his hand on the doorknob. Miguel needed mental prep time. Wardrobe and makeup had still to be done before going onstage at 9:00. Miguel shook his head and stared down at the floor. Luis closed the door.

No time to think about this now. He had a show to do.

Chapter Twenty-Three

Bette twisted her hands nervously as she and Diggy sat waiting in the Club Marbella lounge. They had tickets for Montana's Saturday night show which was about to start. But no sign of Zara or Dave.

"Here comes your G and T luv," said Diggy, as the waiter approached. "Should help calm you down. Go on, get that down you." He tried his best to remain calm, his years of military service gracing him with a steely surface. Jorge had brought them to the hotel early this afternoon. They didn't really expect Zara back until dinnertime, but when dinner had come and gone, Bette began to worry.

"What if they've broke down on the road, or had an accident, or…oh God, been victims of a drive-by?" she fretted, her imagination escalating her fear.

"They've got cell phones, haven't they? We'd have heard if they was in trouble," Diggy said. "Don't get yer knickers in a twist just yet, luv. Drink your drink and let's enjoy the show."

*

The dirt and dust in her mouth made Zara choke as she

tried to breathe in. She coughed and spat out mud and saliva, trying not to swallow. She lay on her side, her cheek flat on the ground. Her face stung as she felt the rough particles rubbing against it. She opened her eyes and tried to raise her hand to wipe the dirt away, but she lay pinned in an awkward position. She tried to gather her whereabouts and squinted to see in the darkness.

Studded with a few early evening stars, the sky above the water still held some light. What seemed like a ten-ton weight lay on top of her. She tried to move her legs and managed to raise her knees a bit. She touched something with her foot. Dave lay unmoving behind her.

His arm still clutched her around her waist. She began to shake, suddenly feeling very cold. And afraid. *Please be alive,* she thought desperately. She moved her feet again, trying to prompt some movement from him. With painful effort, she lifted his arm enough to break his grip.

This got a response and she sighed with relief. He was okay. At least not dead. He let go and miraculously rolled away from her and sat up.

She twisted onto her back, feeling rocks and concrete chunks shift beneath her. They'd made it halfway to the water before the building collapsed. What remained of the structure now lay in a dark heap, its' outline barely discernable against the deepening sky. Rubble lay all around. Somehow, they'd managed to get clear of it.

Her left arm hurt like hell. Dave started to cough and she reached for him in the darkness with her right hand.

"Jesus," she heard him swear, and then spoke her name. "Zara…" Her hand made contact and he grabbed it, turning towards her. She could hear the tumbling of rocks and debris as he moved. He followed her arm up to the shoulder and took hold of it. "Are you okay?" He coughed some more.

"I think so," she said, surprised to find her voice at all. "You?" She heard him spit into the rocks off to his left.

"Yeah," came the one-word response, but nothing more. She had a feeling it wasn't really the truth. She tried sitting up, but her left arm wouldn't cooperate.

"Pull," she said, nudging her right arm against him. He pulled and she sat up. In the moonlight, she could see part of his face. Thank God, they were both still alive. "Are you hurt?" He didn't answer. "Dave," she prodded. More silence. "Dave, answer me," she demanded, raising her voice.

"Huh?" As if he hadn't heard her properly. Something was horribly wrong.

"Are you hurt?" she repeated.

"I don't know." He sat very still. Damn, her left arm hurt. She would have to try and stand, get them moving if she could.

"Can you stand?" she asked. He leaned forward, pulling her with him. She manoeuvred her feet underneath her and pushed up with her legs. Together they managed to rise to their feet. She wrapped her right arm around his neck. He steadied her with an arm around her back.

"What happened," he asked. Zara really didn't know but remembered a sensation, like an electric shock, just before the noise. A premonition. As if her brain knew what was coming even if her body didn't.

"It sounded like an explosion. Or maybe an earthquake."

"How did we get here," he asked next. Worry flooded her brain. He wasn't talking right, his voice sounded muffled. He didn't seem to remember what just happened. Wincing with pain, she put her left arm up over his shoulder to steady them both and touched his face with her right hand. It came away slick and wet with blood. She moved her hand up over his forehead and around the back of his head, feeling for a wound. The entire left side of his head felt warm and slippery.

"Ouch," he pushed her hand away.

"Oh God," she said, her voice trailing away. *Something must have hit him in the head. How bad?* "C'mon, let's get to the water."

He didn't say anything. They moved towards the water's edge, Zara thankful they could walk. Her mind raced. He seemed disoriented, lethargic. He might have a concussion. The salt water would help stop the bleeding and keep him conscious. At the least, it would wash the blood and dirt away. She remembered him more or less tackling her as they ran out from under the falling concrete. He had probably saved them both. They got to the water and waded in up to Zara's waist.

"What are you doing..." he said, sounding dazed. She couldn't tell exactly where the blood oozed from. The waves slapped against her ribs. Far enough. She stopped and faced him squarely.

"Okay, sweetie, we're going to duck under the water for a sec. On three, okay…one, two, three." She pushed down on his shoulders as best she could with her bad arm and under they went.

Her face stung in the salt water. Wherever they were cut, the salt would tell them.

They burst out of the water, Dave yelling in pain, holding his hand to the side of his head. She followed his arm up to the spot and could feel some swelling there.

"What the fuck are you doing," he swore.

"I'm sorry, baby, I'm sorry," she said, knowing he was hurting. "I just need to keep you awake, okay…we can get out of the water now, let's go." They sloshed their way back onto the shore and sat down out of reach of the waves. She held him tight as she could and felt herself starting to cry. "Okay Thunder Boy, snap out of it, I need your help here." He was shivering, but reached over and held her head in his hands.

"I'm okay, shhhh…stop it now," he stroked her hair, brushing it away from her face. "Shhh, it's okay. I feel better, thanks. Boy, you sure know how to throw cold water on a guy."

She started to shake with relief. Now she knew he was okay--he was cracking jokes again. She laughed weakly through her tears, holding her aching arm.

"Let's see that arm," he asked.

"It hurts." He felt it up and down. She gasped in pain when he closed his hand around her forearm.

"You may have broken it," he said. She nodded, but there was nothing for it. Neither spoke for a few minutes. Then Dave said, "I don't think it was an earthquake. That felt like a bomb going off."

Zara took a deep breath. "I think someone's just tried to kill us."

"We've got to call somebody; do you have your cell phone?"

Shit, she thought. *In my bag, but where's the bag?*

"My bag," she said and started back towards where they'd fallen, groping around for it. By sheer luck, her hand touched the smooth surface of the red handbag and snatched it up. Dave came up beside her as she rummaged through it, going by feel. She reached into the pocket where the Blackberry should have been.

It came apart in pieces in her hand.

"No...shit, no!" She flung the pieces across the wreckage. "It's toast."

"My phone's in the truck. We'll have to get back there," Dave said.

She knew he was right. They would need water soon, too. She'd stowed some bottled water in the truck. Slowly, they started westward along the dark, deserted shoreline.

CHAPTER TWENTY-FOUR

Now he had intentionally done murder. This thought weighed heavily on Bernardo. First the woman on the balcony, now the Flynn girl and her partner. The ghosts of his faith began to dance forbiddingly in the back of his mind. Would he be condemned to purgatory? He forced the thoughts away.

He should contact Verrera; let him know the trigger had been pulled and that he could present the bid again. With the papers signed, he could do away with Verrera too and assume the identity of the mysterious Mr. Rodriguez.

Yes, he thought. *That's the answer.* If anyone had seen him, or in any way connected him with the explosion, Bernardo Cruz would be the scapegoat. He must become Rodriguez as soon as possible.

He turned the car around and headed east. All the documents and ID were in the office in Malaga. Once there, he could ditch the vehicle and go elsewhere, anywhere and Cruz would cease to exist. He felt a pang of regret at this but regretted even more that he and Michelle would never be together again.

*

Ignacio felt the tears streaming down his face. Just when he thought things were going right, they had again taken an evil turn. Even if Carmella divorced him, he wouldn't care so much about that as the thought he might lose his children. What to do now, where to go. To Maria's? She'd already warned him to make a change and he had brushed her off.

He could think of only one place. His downtown office.

No cars filled the parking lot, no lights illuminated the building. He parked the car and went to the entry keypad at the main doors. The device buzzed green after he punched the code and went inside. He crossed to the elevators, rubbing his palms together. A cold sweat covered his body.

He rode up the seven floors in the government building as he had done every day for twenty years. The steps to the planning & development office from the elevator landing were mechanical now. He sometimes never recalled walking the distance between them.

He again input a code into a keypad and entered the outer office. He didn't bother turning any lights on for he knew the way by instinct, moving down the hall from the reception area and into his personal office. He felt for the edge of his desk and slumped into his chair. Breaking down, he laid his head on his desk and blubbered in misery, cursing his luck and his situation.

After awhile, when his emotions had been spent and his tears dried, he sat with his head down feeling completely empty. He had no concept of how long he stayed like this; it might have been hours or minutes. Then he heard a noise.

Someone else was coming into the front office.

How could this be? On a Saturday night, of all days to come here, what were the odds of someone else dropping by? He remained quiet, seated at his desk. The intruder might be a cleaning lady who would be gone as quickly as she'd come.

He heard footsteps crossing the reception area, but no

lights switched on. No noise to indicate a cleaning cart or other equipment. The steps came to a stop outside his open office door. The doorknob across the hall began to turn. Cruz' office. *What the devil is going on?* he thought. *What is Cruz doing here?*

The office light flipped on. He could see Bernardo entering the room, dressed in casual clothes. He went to his desk, took a key from his pocket and opened one of the drawers. The same as Verrera's, the government-issue desk had only one drawer with a lock on it, the bottom left. Did Cruz keep booze in there? Drugs? No, he pulled out some papers and sorted through them.

Ignacio stood up and quietly went to the door to confront him. He'd expected to hear from him by now, anyway. He appeared from the shadows to stand squarely in the entrance of Cruz' office. Bernardo didn't seem to notice him at first, but when he glanced inadvertently to the doorway, he jumped almost a foot in the air. The folders he held slipped from his hand and scattered everywhere.

Cruz stumbled backward in fright, tripping over his chair and losing his balance. Verrera almost felt sorry for him. He hadn't intended to scare the living daylights out of his assistant. But neither of them were exactly in a place they should have been.

"Bernardo, what's going on?" Verrera asked. He stooped to pick up the items that had landed nearest him.

Cruz scrambled to get up. "Mierda," he shouted. "¿Qué coño haces aquí?"

Verrera crouched down, staring at the documents in his hands. A passport and a driver's license. They bore Cruz' photo and the name Salvatore Rodriguez. He felt frozen to the spot, though his face burned.

He'd been double-crossed.

Cruz would have taken all his hard work, all his careful

planning and stolen his future from him. The ungrateful, skinny little bastardo! Verrera stayed still, but peered at Bernardo from the corner of his eye.

"¿Qué coño haces aquí? What the hell are you doing here," Cruz repeated.

Slowly, Ignacio stood; a murderous look in his eye as he turned his gaze on him. They stared each other down for only a second before Cruz swept all the items from his desktop at Verrera, then launched himself over the desk and hurtled through the doorway.

A small man, Ignacio could easily have overpowered Bernardo if he'd caught hold of him. As it was, the wiry Cruz ran for the exit leaving Verrera, overweight and ten years older, woefully behind in pursuit.

When Verrera got outside the office, he heard the slamming of the stairwell doors. If no one else entered the building, the elevator should still be stopped on this floor, he reasoned. Ignacio pressed the button and the elevator doors slid open on command.

He pressed M, not knowing where or how Cruz might have entered the building. More than one set of doors existed on main. But with only one parking lot, surely Cruz would have seen Verrera's car. Therefore, he hadn't come through the front. He still held the IDs in his hands as the elevator descended.

Did it matter if he caught up with Cruz? He had the evidence right here. He couldn't exactly turn him in. What could he charge him with, committing fraud more cleverly than his boss?

Only one course of action presented itself. Despite the unfortunate circumstances, Ignacio found himself smiling as the seed of a new plan took root.

CHAPTER TWENTY-FIVE

At last, they could see the lightposts marking the viewpoint where they'd parked the truck. It took a lot longer, in the dark and injured, to return to it than it had to walk to El Mirador from it this afternoon.

Zara had lost track of time, focusing only on reaching the truck, the cell phone, the bottles of water and getting back to Marbella. Or a hospital, whichever they passed first.

She felt sure she'd broken her left arm above the wrist, or at least severely sprained it. Dave seemed to be okay but she worried how much blood he might still be losing, or God forbid, if there might be brain injury.

"How ya doing?" she asked him, checking the bump on his head to see if the bleeding had stopped. "There's the truck, up there."

"I see it. I'm not worried about me, how's that arm?"

"Hurts," she said. "Broken bones are simple. Brain cells are not. Keep talking to me okay, so I know you're alright."

"It's no big deal, it's not the first time," he said.

"What do you mean?" They walked a few more steps.

"I've had a concussion before."

"When?"

"I used to play hockey for MIT. I've had my bell rung a few times."

"Oh." That explained a lot, especially the deer antlers in his office. They were almost at the path to the viewpoint. Finally, they arrived at the truck and in the lamplight took stock of their condition.

"Oh babe, your face," he said sadly, seeing the skin scraped away across her cheekbone. He cradled her arm in his hands. A blackish-red swelling showed from elbow to wrist.

"Let me see," she said, looking for the gash on his head. Hidden by his hair, the bleeding had stopped, but he definitely needed stitches.

He pulled the keys from his pocket.

"Maybe I should drive?" Zara said.

"If I faint, you have permission to take over," he replied, opening the doors and fishing the cell phone out of the glove compartment. He called the local emergency number to report the explosion and then called Jorge, asking him to meet them at the hospital in Marbella.

He started the engine and pulled out onto the highway.

*

The stage lights flashed and the crowd went crazy as the pit band played the intro to the song they'd all come to hear. The screams grew louder as they recognized Montana's current Latin chartbuster, *Una vida por mi*, 'One Life for Me.'

Miguel advanced to centre stage, holding his arms high. Girls tried to rush the stage, held back by the beefy security guards surrounding it. Dressed all in white again, he flashed his brilliant smile to the crowd and basked in their adoration. Motioning for the audience to clap to the beat, he waited teasingly. And when sufficiently ramped up, he stepped to the microphone and began to sing.

"Una vida, un amor por mí,
a cantar y ser libre, La canción me sostiene,
Una vida, un amor por mí"

*One life, one love for me,
to sing and be free, the song will carry me,
one life, one love for me.*

From his tiny vantage point wedged between instrument cases deep in the backstage, Bernardo listened to the words he knew by heart, as he did most of Montana's compositions.

He'd topped 150k on the motorway from Malaga. With his future crumbling around him, he felt desperate to be near Michelle no matter the cost, no matter whether she was man or woman tonight. For she was both and neither.

From a loading bay in the rear of the hotel, he'd managed to enter the backstage area undetected. He knew the layout well but sat frozen in his hiding place, feeling alone, afraid and trapped. Hiding from himself and what might lie ahead. Where was he to go now?

Bette sat in her seat, clapping to the rhythm of *Una vida para mi*. Though one of her favourite numbers, she wasn't enjoying it tonight. She worried about Zara. She and Dave had not returned by show time and at Diggy's insistence, they went ahead into the auditorium to take her mind off them.

Forty-five minutes into the performance, Bette couldn't sit still any longer. She told Diggy she would be back in a few minutes and left the theatre. She returned to their room and setting her handbag on the bed, saw the message button flashing on the house phone. She dived for it.

Jorge's voice stated he was leaving immediately to meet Miss Zara and Mr. Parker at the Medicentre in Marbella, that there had been an incident and would explain later. Zara had requested he contact the Ridleys, tell them the situation and not to worry. They would return to the Club as soon as they could.

Knowing they were at the Medicentre did nothing to ease Bette's anxiety. If anything, it made it worse. She mixed herself a short G and T and sat down to drink it. The gin hit the spot and she visibly relaxed after a few belts. Polishing off the drink she rose to leave but stopped just short of the door, as though she'd forgotten something. She dug into her suitcase until she found it. Tucking it in her handbag, she left the room.

*

Dave lay face down on the treatment bed, chin on his elbows. Dr. Mendez, the on-call physician, sutured the lacerated skin on his head.

"Do you have a headache now?" Mendez asked.

"A little. Not bad."

"Can you say your name, last, first and middle?"

Dave sighed. "Parker, David Justin."

"And can you count backwards from twenty, please?" Dave hesitated. "I apologize if these questions sound foolish," Mendez continued. "It is only a precaution."

"20, 19, 18, 17 . . . ."

"Muy bien, that's fine," the doctor said, satisfied that Dave was all right for the moment. "If the headache persists, please take an analgesic. If they become severe you should come back and see me, is that clear?"

"Yes."

"I see someone is worried about you," Mendez commented as he dabbed the wound with an antiseptic gel. "You can sit up now."

Dave sat up, just in time to see the duty nurse parking a wheelchair at the end of the room. In the chair sat Zara, her forearm in a cast and a butterfly bandage on her cheek.

"Hey," she said.

"Hey, yourself. What's with the wheels? "

"They just like to be careful. From now on, I'm never going to turn down a free ride."

He gestured to her arm. "Broken?"

"I have a 'nondisplaced linear fracture,' she recited. "Pretty minor, considering." She turned to Dr. Mendez. "How many stitches did he need?"

The doctor held up five fingers. "You are both very lucky to have such minor injuries. Mr. Parker has some bruising and two cracked ribs, but the head wound should heal nicely," Mendez said, nodding. He glanced from one to the other. "Oh yes, since he has a history of previous concussion, it would be wise to have someone stay the night with him. Can that be arranged?"

"Yes," they said simultaneously. Mendez raised his eyebrows, and said "Buenas noches," as he left the room. Dave stood and went over to kneel beside Zara's chair.

"You look a little worse for wear. How do you feel?"

"Tired, mostly. Sore." Dave nodded and looked into her eyes. It broke his heart to see her in pain, bandaged up like this. He thought about what she'd said earlier.

"You said, 'someone just tried to kill us.' Do you still feel that way?" She bit her lip, then nodded. "And are you going to tell the police that?"

"Not yet. It's just a feeling."

"So far, your feelings have been pretty accurate. That look on your face, right before we booked it out of there, what were you feeling then?" She thought about it for a moment.

"Electricity," she said. "Like lightning going through my body. As if my brain was receiving the detonator signal and telling me to run."

Dave shook his head slowly from side to side. "Weird. You saved our asses, you know that," he said.

She looked at him steadily. "I wouldn't have made it out

fast enough if you hadn't been with me." He took her hand, kissed it and stood up, chuckling out loud.

"What a team. Lightning Girl and Thunder Boy," he announced. Zara laughed too, even though it hurt. They turned to leave and saw Jorge in the doorway.

"You are both OK?" he asked. They nodded. "It is almost midnight. David, I think it's best you leave the truck here and I will take you both back to the Club. I'm sure we can arrange a room for you. Also, the police say they want to interview you both tomorrow. Shall we go?"

With Dave's arm around her, they made their way out.

CHAPTER TWENTY-SIX

The concert ended at 11:30. Bette and Diggy paced nervously in the lobby of Club Marbella, waiting for Zara. They weren't the only ones waiting. Separated by several metres, Luis and Raoul installed themselves casually about the room. Wearing street clothes, they had been tailing the Ridleys ever since they entered the theatre.

The automatic entrance doors slid open and Bette's eyes fixed on the threshold until at last she glimpsed Jorge entering the lobby with Dave and Zara close behind. Dave held Zara, her arm in a sling, as they walked. Bette fairly ran to them, her pink heels clattering across the marble floor.

"Ye Gods, what's happened to the pair of you?" She went to hug Zara, uncertain of how to put her arms about her without disturbing the sling. Diggy stood behind Bette, equally concerned.

"It's a long story," said Zara, reaching out to Bette with the uninjured arm. Diggy shook Jorge's hand saying, "Good man, rescuing our kids, thanks for ringing us." He turned to Dave and slapped him on the shoulder. "You're a sight, lad, I knew you'd protect our girl."

"We should have just come back all together," Zara said to Bette. "I'm so sorry we worried you."

Jorge stepped in. "Sr. & Sra. Ridley, we should let them get some rest now. You can all talk over coffee in the morning."

Diggy held up a hand. "Of course, you're totally right, mate. We's just so happy to see you safe and sound. Sort of," he added, pointing to their bandages.

Happy to see the Ridleys too, Zara clung to Bette with her good arm, reassuring her she was all right, when she spotted them over Bette's shoulder.

"What's wrong, dear?" Bette said, feeling Zara stiffen.

"It's 007," she whispered. Bette whirled around. Luis and Raoul approached them swiftly.

"Miss Zara Flynn," Luis said in a low voice. Zara stared them down and as they came a little too close for Dave's liking, he stepped in front of her.

"Can I help you gentlemen," Dave said, in a most unfriendly tone. They both sent him a condescending look.

"Step aside, vaquero; we have information for the lady."

"From whom," Zara said sharply.

"I think you know who," Luis said. Dave looked over his shoulder at Zara. Her face expressionless, Bette stood fast next to her.

Luis relaxed his stance. "Bring el vaquero if you wish. Es importante, for your safety."

Dave scowled at the cowboy reference. He kept his eyes on Zara, seeing what she wanted to do.

"Me and all," Bette said. Luis shrugged and waved them forward. Zara stood still, thinking at light speed. As attractive as the prospect of seeing Miguel again would have been just a few days ago, the situation was very different now. What information could these two possibly have? Why would they be concerned about her safety? They didn't insist she come alone this time.

There must be something else going on, she decided. However, she refused to go to the penthouse again. Perhaps they'd be willing to meet on neutral ground if the matter was so important. Something told her she should leave Dave behind, too. Not because it might be awkward, but so she could call for backup if anything went wrong.

"Who are these guys and how do they know you," Dave said, impatience in his voice. Zara put her hand on his shoulder, whispered something to him and slipped him her cardkey. Then she spoke to Luis.

"Listen, we've had a really long day, we're tired and we're grouchy. Can we do this somewhere neutral, maybe the lounge?"

Luis considered this. He nodded to Raoul, who turned away and began using his headset. In a moment, he finished his call and said, "We can use the backstage, we'll meet you there." Raoul turned and left.

Luis took over. "This way, please." Zara took Bette by the hand.

"Come with me?" she asked.

"Too right, I will." To Diggy she said, "You stay put, luv." The two women followed Luis toward the theatre.

As they moved out of view, Dave turned to Jorge. "She wants you to give me your cell phone. We lost hers, but she has mine with her and can call me if there's any trouble. Mr. Ridley, she said you'd explain who those guys were."

Diggy crossed his arms and watched the ladies disappear around the corner. "I'm not exactly sure," he admitted. "But they work for the Latin loverboy, Mickey Mountain."

Dave and Jorge looked at him blankly.

"Miguel Montana, the singer," Diggy went on. "He's been performing here all this week. We saw his show tonight; was a right good one, too. He took a bit of a shine to our Zara after Tuesday's show, that's when them two blokes turned up."

"She's met this guy before?" Dave asked, his voice hardening. Diggy uncrossed his arms, patted Dave on the shoulder.

"Take it easy now lad, nothing happened, according to her. She's safe with our Bette playing watchdog. When you've been with a missus as long as I have, you learn when to trust. You'll learn, too."

*

Zara felt too exhausted to be frightened. She just needed to find out what they wanted from her. She and Bette followed Luis through the theatre and around to the backstage area. They stepped around electrical cords, light banks and spot stands, packing crates and folded risers. In a clear area, Luis pulled out some stacking chairs and offered them a seat. He put his hand to his headset, listening.

"They will just be a few moments," he affirmed. Bette sat nervously as Zara recounted what had happened since morning. How they'd almost been killed and couldn't shake the feeling that it had all been planned. And that Miguel somehow had related information. She discreetly showed Bette the cell phone in her hand. Bette nodded, but looked doubtful that a phone would offer much protection.

Raoul returned. Behind him, dressed in the same plain gray hoodie to hide his face, walked Miguel. As they came closer, Zara recognized the same pleasant scent he'd worn the other night.

Miguel fixed his eyes on her, a look of concern on his face when he saw her arm. Bette nearly swooned, catching in her breath as she glimpsed the famous rock star up close and personal.

"Miss Zara, what has happened to you, are you alright?"

"Your…friends...say you have information for me," Zara said. Miguel looked from her, to Luis, to Bette.

He spoke in a soft voice filled with regret. "I apologize for this intrusion. It is good you have brought someone who loves you, *Cherie*. Life is nothing without love. There is strength in love."

It seemed a lifetime ago that Zara sat facing him in the penthouse. He appeared even more handsome now, as he exposed this genuine and vulnerable side of himself.

"I think someone is trying to kill me," Zara said. "Do you know anything about this?" He sat down in the chair opposite her and reached for her good hand. She took it and waited.

"You are in danger. I see that he has already tried to reach you," Miguel said, touching her bandaged face. "It is my fault. He is here because of me."

"Who is here," she asked. "Who?"

Miguel sighed in anguish. "I call him El Ángel Oscuro, Dark Angel. But his name is Cruz. Do you know him?"

Zara searched her mind for that name. Then she remembered the skinny man at Mondays' meeting. *Why would he be involved?*

"I think so. Why am I in danger? What will he do?"

"He came to your room on the tenth floor. But you were not there. He didn't know you had moved. Someone he thought was you fell to her death from the balcony. At his hands. I don't know the reason, but perhaps you do."

Drained, she couldn't sort out anything logical in her mind. She vaguely remembered Cruz, an assistant to the Planning officer. She clasped Miguel's hand tighter.

"No. I don't. I only met him once." She forced herself to think harder. *It must be to do with El Mirador.* She visualized the quiet, odd sort of man. Kept his hands in his pockets. "How do you know him?" she asked.

Miguel displayed an enigmatic smile. "Let us say, I *know* him. He is not pleased with me right now. He is…a jealous person. And he means to kill you. It is only suerte, luck, that he didn't succeed the first time," he said, gesturing to her sling. "You will know him by a tattoo on the back of his hand. A tiny angel in black ink. Be warned, I have not seen Ángel since yesterday. He may still be here, or he may not. He is dangerous."

Zara looked at him as though for the last time and leaned towards him.

"Thank you. And I apologize for...not being very good company."

Miguel smiled. "De nada, Zara Flynn. It is enough that we are friends, yes? I am glad." He looked up at Bette, then back to Zara. "You should go now." He stood and held out his hand to Bette. She eagerly placed her hand in his and he kissed it in knightly fashion. "Take care."

He turned towards his bodyguards and with a loud snapping sound, the room went black.

*

Bernardo waited by the electrical panel, listening for movement. He'd watched them the entire time, crouched in his hiding spot since the performance. He couldn't believe his eyes. What was she doing still alive, the bitch? He knew their positions, but they didn't know his. He would move straight for Flynn. The others didn't matter. He could escape before they found the light switches.

Luis and Raoul immediately assumed their prime responsibility, seizing Miguel and moving to the exit. Their training made it second nature to have memorized the layout of any area their client entered.

This left Bette and Zara unprotected. Bette's chair scraped the floor, as if getting up to run. Deathly tired and with her arm throbbing, Zara didn't want to move at all. Better to wait until someone restored the lights.

In that moment what felt like a bulldozer hit her from the

side, knocking her chair over and sending her hard to the floor. Someone dragged her by the arm across the bare wooden surface. She screamed, swung and kicked her legs trying to wrench loose from her attacker. Suddenly her arm jerked free and she rolled away overtop of her cast, mindless of the pain. She fumbled for Dave's cell phone and hit the recall for Jorge's number.

She felt a hard kick to her ribs and for a moment thought she might vomit from the pain.

*

After sending food and water up to suite 514, Dave joined Jorge and Diggy in the late night bar. He felt ready to collapse, but out of his mind with worry over Zara and Bette. He ran his hands through his matted hair, wincing as he grazed the bump on his head. Diggy ordered beer for all three of them.

Dave told them all he could remember about the explosion, how they'd escaped and how Zara felt they were being targeted. They nursed their pints, not particularly enjoying them under the circumstances. The three sat silent for a few minutes until Jorge spoke up.

"You care deeply for Miss Zara, yes?' Dave raised his head to give Jorge a pained look that said it all. Jorge nodded as if confirming a fact he already knew too well. "I could feel it when we talked the other day. I knew you were the right one."

Diggy added his two cents. "Flaming hell, the only one what didn't know that right off was the lass herself. But she's mad for you too, lad. Anyone can see it just by looking at the pair of you."

The three men nearly jumped when the cell phone went off in Dave's pocket. He grabbed for it, flipped it open and felt his blood run cold at the ungodly noise coming from it. Amid the cacophony of shouts and screams were gunshots. He was across the room before Diggy could shout to the bartender, "Call security!"

*

Shots rang out what seemed like only a few feet ahead as he charged into the dark, cluttered backstage. Fear spiked in Dave's brain. *Dear God no, no, no, NO! Please let her be safe, away from whatever crazed bastard fired that weapon.* He dropped to a crouch at the sound, hoping to find something, anything, to take out the sick son of a bitch. Another gunshot from the opposite direction and then footsteps running, crashing into God knew what in the darkness.

Diggy found the panel and one section of lights came on. A final shot dropped a body to the floor, frighteningly close to where Zara lay curled in a foetal position.

The victim, a smallish man, neither of the two from the lobby, sprawled awkwardly barely a metre from her. Only a little farther away and holding it in a curiously expert stance stood Bette, pointing a handgun at the body. Dave blinked at the bizarre scene and felt his stomach start to lurch.

The lights came fully up as security guards swarmed in and ringed the area where Zara lay. Sick with relief, Dave knelt beside her, unsure if he should try to move her. Despite the maddening chaos, the cavernous room seemed to shrink around him, vacuuming out all sound as it did so.

The visual images in front of him grew in intensity and he saw everything in acute detail. Her shuddering body curled up next to him. Jorge huddled over her on the other side. The crumpled form of the man felled by a bullet just inches away, his left arm stretched out on the floor and the black mark on the back of his hand oddly conspicuous.

As if seen through a zoom lens the black mark filled Dave's field of vision, enlarging the tiny winged angel to enormous proportions. In a moment of blank clarity he relived sitting in the airport lounge in Jakarta, waiting for his flight, when the little man in the suede jacket stepped next to him at the bar. His gaze fixed on the unusual design on the back of his hand. Still feeling a bit trippy from his meds he'd said to him, "Sweet tattoo, man."

The image rolled up and away like a window blind and Dave slipped back into the present, hovering over his terrified girl.

He laid his fingers at the side of her throat and exhaled silent thanks at feeling a strong pulse. She opened her eyes, then closed them again and began to tremble and sob uncontrollably.

"Take me out of here," she begged, in between ragged breaths. Dave's ears seemed to flood with noise and heard what seemed like hundreds of voices all speaking at once with only a few random words piercing through the muddle. 'Policía, custodia, espere aquí.'

Then his own voice, "Do what you have to, but I'm taking her." He lifted her in his arms and she clung to him like life itself. She buried her face in his chest and cried like a baby.

CHAPTER TWENTY-SEVEN

On Sunday, church bells rang throughout Marbella and beyond, as they did every Sunday in Spain. Zara sat in the local police station giving her account of the previous day's events.

The body removed from the Club Marbella theatre had been identified as Bernardo Dominic Cruz. Listed as a public servant for the municipality of Malaga under the supervision of Ignacio Verrera, Cruz had no prior police record. He also appeared on the registered guest list at the Club Marbella.

Police were dispatched to El Mirador after receiving Dave's call about the explosion. Evidence supported the use of explosive charges and a search of Cruz' vehicle found a detonator device concealed within an empty laptop case. Verrera would be sought as a person of interest in the case.

"Can Mrs. Ridley be released?" Zara asked. The detective shuffled papers into a file folder. "Si, Miss Flynn. Sra. Ridley's firearm had the proper licensing and appears to have been fired in self-defence. She is free to go. We will be in touch if we require more information. Buenas Días." He rose from behind his desk, as did Zara with a little help from Dave. The two of them walked out into the bright daylight.

"You did great in there, babe," he said, his arm around her shoulders. He kissed her bandaged cheek. "How do you feel?"

"Like I need a vacation," she said. "Somehow bombs and gunfire just seem to take it out of me." They laughed together, standing in the police station parking lot. A strong breeze came off the waterfront, blowing Zara's hair across her face. She pulled him to her with her good arm and kissed him lightly on the lips. "I was supposed to be watching over you last night. Instead you rescued me, again."

Exhausted, they'd spent the rest of the night in Zara's room. They woke up locked in each other's embrace still fully dressed.

"Well, I'll let it go this time," he said. "But you owe me." They walked to the Flynn truck, retrieved from the Medicentre earlier. "I talked to Ernie." Dave said. "The reports will be in tomorrow."

"Oh, Ernesto," Zara said, thinking how bad this all sounded. "He's got a mess on his hands, I'll bet he wasn't pleased with us."

"No. But he's glad we're safe. We'll have some explaining to do when we get back to the office." He held her close and rested his head on her shoulder. "I need to go home for awhile, get cleaned up," he said. "Can I come back for you, have dinner together?"

"Well, like you said, we both need to be at work tomorrow. You needn't drive all the way back for me."

He released her, only to grip her by the shoulders and give her an admonishing look. "I don't intend to spend tonight or any other night of my life without you, Lightning Girl. Get used to it. Pick you up at six."

Zara looked at him, drinking in the image of him so she could never forget how he looked at that very moment. She adored him. She didn't want to be apart from him, either. Not one minute. Her heart was full.

"In that case," she said, "why don't I stay at your place? I'll talk Jorge into loaning me the Mercedes. What are you cooking tonight?" He tightened his arms around her waist and lifted her into the air, kissing her madly. The pain from his cracked ribs seemed inconsequential.

Reluctantly he dropped her off at the Club, making sure she had his address and her promise to be there by six or he'd have her arrested. She wanted to say goodbye to the Ridleys and see them off before their four o'clock flight.

More than that, she needed to thank Bette for saving her life. Who knew this flamboyant, middle-aged Englishwoman was a practiced sharpshooter? She shook her head at the strange turn of events. As she made her way through the lobby, a man waved to her from his seat on one of the overstuffed couches. It was Mr. Verrera.

"Senorita Flynn, I am sorry to intrude like this." He stood to greet her, holding his briefcase in one hand. He stared at her arm, minus the sling but still in its cast and the bandage on her face. "I need to speak with you."

"The police are looking for you," she confided. "I won't tell them I've seen you."

"Gracias. It appears my assistant was working against me. And you. He tried to defraud you of your property under a false company name. I am sorry for the trouble he caused. Are you certain you're alright?"

He seemed sincere and truly concerned about her. "Si, Sr. Verrera. It looks worse than it is," she said, raising the arm a little. "But I'll be fine. I was lucky. Your assistant, not so much. He's dead." He looked at her and nodded, his expression unreadable. "I'm not sure we'll be able to proceed with the restoration plans you approved. It may be awhile before any decision or progress is made."

"It is of no importance now, Miss. You see, I will be leaving my job here and going away. I have some other opportunities that have presented themselves. I wanted to make sure you were all right and wish you well in your endeavours. And thank you again for...not seeing me," he said with a slight grin.

"De nada," she replied. He took her good hand and kissed the back of it gallantly.

Àdios, Sta. Flynn. Buena suerte." His cell phone beeped in his pocket. With a nod, he took his leave.

Verrera put the phone to his ear as he began to turn away and after a moment, Zara saw him smiling. *"Si, this is Rodriguez,"* she heard him reply.

*

Not large, Dave's apartment had a great open-concept space and a terrific skyline view. The Mediterranean exposed itself intermittently beyond the downtown towers. When Zara arrived, he stopped her at the door and stepped out into the hallway.

Carrying her inside, he kicked the door shut and set her down on the couch where a frosty margarita pitcher waited on a side table. They toasted and Zara savoured the salty crystals on the rim of her glass.

She wore a short, black and white print dress, with skinny spaghetti straps that showed off her neck and shoulders that were just beginning to sport a tan. Dave decided against a shirt altogether, going for comfort in a pair of favorite board shorts. As Zara looked around the place, she saw something familiar. Two guitars sat side by side in their stands against one wall--one acoustic and one electric.

"I presume you play?" she said.

"Once in a while, when I can't sleep, sometimes."

"I bet your neighbours appreciate that. Would you play something, now?"

"Sure, if you'd like." He picked up the acoustic and sat down on the couch, tuning it before strumming a few introductory chords. He played softly while they sipped their drinks "You figured it out, didn't you…what's underneath El Mirador. You were trying to tell me something." Dave said.

She'd hashed things over in her mind what seemed like a thousand times since yesterday. One thing she felt absolutely certain of.

"The smell," she said. "It's very distinctive, raw bitumen. There's a lot of it out west. My class went on an exchange trip one year to the tar sands. It smells exactly like that. When we were at the site on Wednesday, I couldn't place it. But the second time, the weather had changed a bit and the wind."

She recognized the tune he was playing and said, "Roundabout."

He smiled, nodding she was correct. "Maybe your senses weren't as sharp that day," he suggested, alluding to her hangover.

"Ah, no." she admitted. "You weren't exactly catching me at my best. But if there's a bitumen deposit under the foundation, of any significance, that means a lot of money to whomever gains mineral rights to the site and can extract it successfully."

"Which right now, happens to be you."

She nodded. "I see now why Dad paid more than market value for it."

Dave had switched to a new tune. "Malaguena," she stated, smiling at him. "Did you know I received an offer to buy it?" He shook his head, but grinned in enjoyment of their impromptu game of name-that-tune.

"A company called Vistamar Holdings faxed in an offer on Monday. For about a quarter of the price, stating it was contaminated and an 'eco-hazard.' They lowballed, to justify the expense of the alleged cleanup. Now I see they planned to clean up, all right. Monetarily, not environmentally."

"I've heard that name, Vistamar Holdings." Dave said,

starting another song. "Ernie gave me their report before we went out on there on Wednesday. They're a small sub company, did surveys for us a few times. I didn't know they were bidding on properties."

Verrera's words began to echo in Zara's mind, '*he tried to defraud you under a false company name.*'

"It was Cruz," she said, a light coming on in her brain. "Cruz was Vistamar Holdings." She listened to the guitar again, pausing to think a little harder about this new tune. Then she pointed to the instrument and said, "Sleepwalk."

He stopped playing and set the guitar back in its stand. "You're good," he said, but his face turned serious. "Cruz was also the one who nearly got us killed." Dave frowned in thought. "Did you see the tattoo on his hand?" he asked.

Zara thought about what Miguel had told her. El Ángel Oscuro. He had some sort of relationship with him. One she didn't want to think about. The most beautiful flower arrangement waited in her room when she returned from the police station. 'Amour toujours, Miguel' the card read. "Yes, I saw it."

"I've seen him before. In the Jakarta airport when I flew out. He ordered a drink from the bar and I saw his tattoo." He regarded her carefully.

Her eyes darkened and in a barely audible voice said, "Go on."

Mindful of her arm in its cast, he came and sat close to her. "He might also have been responsible for your father's death," he said, sounding reluctant to speak the words that he knew must be spoken.

Zara's throat went dry. Dave's words were logical, but it didn't matter much now. Tristan was gone and she would have to make her peace with that. She nodded in agreement.

"So the only question left is the one you wanted answered most," Dave said. "Why Tristan left El Mirador to you and what did he expect from you." She looked into his eyes. If they had been two cobalt-blue oceans, Zara would have dived in headfirst.

"I don't know," her voice squeaked. "I wish he could tell me."

He put his arm around her, kissed her forehead and stroked her hair. The only comfort he could offer was his presence. For the moment, it was enough. She leaned against him in silence.

After a minute or two he reminded her, "Hey, we haven't eaten yet. Hope you like clam chowder." This made her smile and brought her back to reality.

"Love it. Not in your average guy's culinary repertoire. Where'd you learn to make it?"

He laughed. "Remember, I lived in Boston. It's a criminal offense there if you don't like crab and clams. And beans."

"Go Bruins," she added with a closed-fist salute. "By the way, what did you get sick with in Indonesia?"

He grabbed her hand and pulled her up off the couch. He tilted his face slowly towards her.

"Food poisoning. Let's eat."

This time her tears were from laughter.

They ate, talked and drank by candlelight for hours, about anything and everything. Particularly interested in the renovations Dave had made to the apartment, she started to ask how he'd managed to alter the joists to achieve the ceiling effect in the room, when he cut her off.

"Okay, Lightning Girl, that's enough shop talk for today." He took her glass from her and set it down. "We'll have plenty of that in the morning." He snuffed out the candles and took her by the hand. They stood silhouetted against the evening sky, the lighted windows of office towers now glittering like stars in the distance.

He led her to the bedroom, his bedroom. She could feel

desire rising inside her, as if she'd been apart from him for days instead of mere hours. It felt so right, being here. In his domain, where she belonged.

They stood in the darkness and he pulled her close, kissing her long and hard. His fingertips traced up her arms, slipping the thin straps off her shoulders and letting the dress fall to the floor. He slid his hands down her back and around her buttocks.

She'd worn nothing at all underneath her dress, as if she'd been waiting for this moment. She could almost feel him burning inside, sending the heated blood rushing to his loins.

"I liked your playing," she said. "Thank you for sharing it with me."

"No problem," he whispered. "Let me know if you can't sleep. It works like a charm."

"I don't want to sleep."

The velcro closure on his shorts made a ripping sound as she pulled it open, pushing the shorts down over his hips until they too, fell to the floor. He stepped out of them, grabbed her behind her thighs and lifted her to him.

"Good," he said. She wrapped her legs around him as he carried her to the bed; the bolts in its steel frame chattering as he fairly flung her onto it.

Caging her with his body, he streaked kisses across her collarbone and over her breasts. Her breathing heightened and her body begged for his touch. "You don't know how much I wanted to get you here," he said. "Get you home."

He licked her nipples and tugged gently at them with his lips, making them tense and harden. Zara thrilled to both his words and his hands. "Home safe…just us. No one else in the world." His whispered words tickled her skin in between kisses.

She wanted him so badly. *No, needed him so badly.* "No… No one else," she echoed, her voice choked with emotion.

He stroked her thighs and they parted, asking for him. He obliged and his fingers again connected with the wet, needy flesh between them, insisting, exploring, demanding.

Zara felt blinded with arousal. She raised her hips in response to him. She wanted to scream out his name, giving his neighbours more than guitar playing to worry about. Instead it left her lips in a throaty purr, "Oh, Dayy-vid..."

She heard him chuckle softly. "Ah, the Goddess speaks..." She wanted to return the mind-blowing pleasure he was giving her and pushed on his shoulder with her free hand to roll him onto his back.

He sprawled leisurely, awaiting whatever erotic delight she had in mind. Her tongue made a straight line down his abdomen to the base of his marvellously erect member and painted the sides of it with the broad strokes of an artists' brush, working her way up its length.

He uttered deep, groaning sighs and he grasped the strands of her hair that swept across his clenched abs. She took him in her mouth and glazed his hard muscle up and down with wet lips.

He accepted her gift. For as long as he could.

Suddenly he gripped her shoulders and pulled her upwards. In a single swift motion he flipped her to one side, landing her on her stomach. "I see I will have to tame the Goddess of Lightning," he said, his voice raspy yet teasing. "...Lest she kill me with her powers."

Goosebumps raised on Zara's skin at the subtle change in his voice. A tingle of anticipation ran through her, something not quite fear, but a feeling she was about to lose all control.

Kneeling upright over her, Dave took hold by her underarms and pulled her forward, yanking her up onto her knees. She let out a gasp of surprise and reached out, grabbing for the steel rail of the headboard.

He reached around and took hold of her breasts in both

hands, his chest tight against her back. He snuggled his chin on her shoulder and whispered in her ear. "Behold, Goddess…"

Zara trembled with excitement. His male force radiated from him like kryptonite, making her feel weak. He fondled her breasts in a thorough, possessive way and she could feel his hipbones pressed against her bottom.

His erection nestled between her cheeks. She bowed her head in blissful surrender.

His hands slid down her front and touched her inner thighs, nudging them further apart. Every hair on her body stood on end as she waited, barely drawing breath, for what would come next.

Both hands met at her crotch, fingers spreading her and reaching inside her folds. Graceful strokes sent thrills rocketing through her and she cried out in meaningless syllables of an unknown language.

His stroking kept on. Mad, incoherent images flashed in her brain. He whispered in her ear again, "Lightning always comes before Thunder…"

"Ah," she choked out something that resembled a laugh, her breath coming in short, rapid intakes. She leaned forward to brace her right hand against the wall, trying to hold out for just a few more seconds. "There…is no thunder without… light…ning…"

He entered her from behind. The dual stimulation made her explode into orgasm. Colors swam behind her closed eyelids, the unspeakable waves of pleasure marauding through her core and extending to every limb.

His hands were on her hips now, steadying her. His first thrust lifted her knees off the surface of the bed. She drew in a shuddering breath. He made a low-pitched sound worthy of a martial-arts move as he pushed into her a second time and then a third.

She'd never felt anything so exquisitely powerful, so

primeval, making her want to succumb to it and to him for all eternity. She felt him tensing for another thrust and she leaned into him as he plunged forward, taking all of what he had to give her.

His arms wrapped around her waist, pulling her against him as he sank back on his knees.

She felt the tremors of his body as he came. He leaned his forehead against the nape of her neck and uttered her name in an almost mournful cry.

"Zara...I love you."

CHAPTER TWENTY-EIGHT

"I miss you, Mom. I'll be so glad to see you," Zara said. She sat at her desk at the Flynn office in Malaga. "We'll be at the airport to pick you up. Safe trip." She paused, listening to her mother's voice. "What? I guess so, sure. Hold on."

She pushed the hold button and looked up at Ernesto standing in her doorway. "My mother will be arriving on Friday," she said. "We'll be taking the weekend to visit family in Zaragoza." Ernesto nodded. "She's asked to talk to you," she said, raising an eyebrow.

Ernesto peered over the top of his eyeglasses and returned the gesture. Smiling, he said, "Muy bien. I'll take it in my office. Come as soon as you're ready."

He still hadn't made his optometrist appointment.

Zara rose from behind her desk, looking sideways at him. "I'm ready now, but I'll give you a few minutes."

If her mother wanted to talk to him, then who was she to question it? She walked into the reception area. Pilar smiled and nodded to her.

"Como esta, Sta. Flynn. How is that arm?"

"Muy bien, gracias," she said. "I should have this cast off in a few weeks."

Dave came into the reception area to see the two of them chatting. "Hola," he said. "Am I interrupting anything?"

"Not for me," replied Pilar. She looked back and forth between them then cast a glance toward the other office girls, whose faces held all the disappointment of unchosen puppies.

Oblivious to them, he nodded at Zara. "Ernie's ready for us, shall we?" He reached out for her hand.

They took a seat at the center table in Ernesto's office. Already present, Chavez stared at the cast on Zara's arm. Ernesto swiveled around, still talking on his phone. He spoke softly in Spanish.

Zara blushed. Roughly translated he'd said, 'Me too, I can't wait. Hurry back, dear friend.' Was he still talking to her mother?

He hung up and turned his attention to the boardroom table but couldn't hide his delighted smile. Zara sent him a wicked look. Ignoring her, he said, "Chavez? Please proceed."

Chavez passed around copies of his analysis. "First off, you should know that the bones we found were not human. Turns out, they were bovine; and random segments at that. Not even from the same area of the animal. Looks like someone dropped them there by accident or as a joke. At any rate, they are not significant. The core samples however, tell us quite a bit more. They contained a great deal of seawater, which caused the unstable texture of the sand. However, the sand itself is actually bitumen, commonly known as heavy crude oil. Tar sands." He paused and glanced around the table.

Dave grinned at Zara. She'd been right on with her assessment.

"Do we know how much is potentially there?" she asked Chavez.

"To determine that would take a more detailed survey. But it's unlikely to be a large deposit. Although fairly common in many countries, only two sites in the world account for

90% of reserves and have sufficient upgrader technology to produce useable oil."

"So, it could remain in place, undeveloped," Ernesto said. Chavez nodded.

"And is it hazardous to leave it in place, from an environmental standpoint?" Zara asked, thinking about the Vistamar report.

"It's a natural resource. The problems exist with its' extraction, not its presence."

"Why would the original structure have been built on it in the first place?" Dave asked.

Chavez shrugged. "Ignorance, probably. The original building footprint was smaller. An addition came later and since they couldn't pour footings in the soft bitumen, they simply built around it. Which explains the absence of columns in that area. The exact cause of the fire though, is still unknown."

Zara shifted in her chair. "I found it on the internet," she said. "The fire occurred in 1972. Official news makes little mention of it, but social network chatter, blogs and community news archives paint a more colourful story. It seems the original owner, Sr. Ariel Torres, intended to burn up his cheating mistress while in bed with her lover right in his own hotel. It burned very quickly, no doubt the petroleum deposit beneath it providing a healthy fuel supply. Unfortunately, Mr. Torres lost his own life in the incident."

"About the explosion on the weekend." Ernesto said. Chavez looked at him, taken aback. He hadn't heard this news. Ernesto turned to Zara, indicating for her to explain.

"I went back to have another look around. I shouldn't have and I didn't intend to get so close, but...as they say," she looked at Ernesto again, "we were in the wrong place at the wrong time. Someone planted explosives and set them off. We were nearly killed," she gestured to the cast on her arm and sent Dave a meaningful look.

He held her gaze steadily. "Tell them your theory," he said.

"Vistamar Holdings falsified the survey on the site, trying to devalue it so they could purchase it cheaply," Zara explained. "Then extract the oil and make a profit."

"How was the explosion triggered, and by whom?" asked Chavez.

"I can't prove it, but I believe the person responsible was involved with Vistamar. This same person murdered one of the clerks at my hotel and then came after me. I think he also set off the explosion in Indonesia." She looked directly at Ernesto. "Bernardo Cruz. He's dead now, also."

Ernesto looked shocked. The room fell silent.

"What happens to the site now?" asked Chavez.

"That's up to Zara," Ernesto said. "But the structure is, for all intents and purposes, destroyed. It must be removed. Mining the area would be a serious undertaking, but is one option. Or?"

Zara stared down at her hands for a moment and then looked up as an idea occurred to her. "Or, we can let nature restore it. Build something else. An interpretive centre, perhaps."

Ernesto smiled. "That's an interesting option."

Zara waved her hand. "I don't know really. The parcel is over 100 hectares, there's room to build more than one thing. There's no hurry."

With that, they adjourned their meeting, Ernesto tasking Chavez with a more detailed survey on the size of the bitumen field. Dave would start arranging crews for the remaining demolition and removal.

He and Zara exchanged knowing glances as they prepared to leave. Ernesto didn't try to hide his satisfied smile as Zara sidled up to him.

"Alright, Sr. Misteriosa, just what are your intentions towards my mother?"

Ernesto blushed in spite of his swarthy complexion. "It is a long story Zara, but I believe it may yet have a happy ending." He smiled, refusing to say more.

She wagged a finger at him but smiled back nonetheless. Her mother would get the third degree from her.

Zara went back to her office. With Marlena arriving by week's end she'd been thinking about her next move. She would have to decide soon. To return to Montreal, be an arms-length CEO? Maybe. A Flynn office operated there. Her friends were all there, her condo, her car. Or stay, as her heart told her to do.

She thought of Dave's words in the parking lot yesterday. *'I don't intend to spend tonight or any other night of my life without you.'*

Would he leave here, come back with her? She couldn't ask that of him. What held her back? Did she miss home? She could always visit. The idea of not being with Dave every day made her feel sick.

Then she remembered something. She pulled open the top drawer of her desk, looking for the portfolio case of Tristan's drawings. As she did so, something slid from the back of the drawer into plain sight.

The small desktop photo frame held a picture of her mother, her arms around a little girl. Herself. It looked like a vacation photo, a smiling Marlena with her dark hair whipping around in the wind. Zara, peering into the camera with the wide eyes of a 5-year-old, clutched her mother's arm.

She turned the frame over, looking for a date or caption. She pulled away the hinged back cover to inspect the back of the print. Jammed between it and the frame backing was a DVD. She teased it out with a fingernail and held it for a moment, realizing with a cold tightening in her stomach that it was meant for her.

Sliding it from its paper sleeve, she inserted it into her computer's optical drive.

The auto-play launched a Flash file. The opening sequence showed an overhead fly-by of open countryside. Flat tundra-like plains, furred with boreal groves of spruce, pine and aspen. The scene transitioned into a panoramic view of a surface mining operation, miles wide, its' gigantic transports lifting masses of dark, claylike clumps to conveyors on their way to steam-assisted processors.

This image dissolved into a disturbing aerial shot of a spewing underwater well, the oil an unwelcome passenger on the waters' surface that advanced steadily upon an unprotected shore. Then followed the heart-wrenching images of waterfowl coated in the brownish sludge, unable to move.

Shifting again, the scene returned to the open spaces of the original frames, this time showing the transformation of a reclaimed tailings pond--its' surface repaired with thick, rich topsoil that fearlessly presented tender new grass shoots and spruce seedlings. Zara knew this place. The great oil sand fields she and her classmates had toured.

The picture changed to a close-up of a pair of gloved hands that gingerly cupped a tiny duckling amid the newly sprouted grass. Panning outwards the crouched, hard-hatted figure holding the creature became visible, lifting his face to the camera and smiling broadly.

Freeze frame.

Zara stared, immobile, at the familiar craggy features of her father's face. Tufts of his still-thick, greying blond hair stuck out from under the hardhat. A voice-over began to play.

To the only women in my life. Marlena, whom
I have loved since that wild day in Zaragoza.
Remember it was all for you. Little Zara, named
for that place, you are not so little now. I know you
wanted to make your own way in the world and I

*will be forever proud of you. Someday you will be my
successor and I have no doubt you will take the torch
and hold it high. I pray you have the joy of children
in your life and can pass it on to them as well.*

*I must place on you a great burden, which I
regret. But you are the only answer. El Mirador
will become your legacy; it has a dark past and
you can bring it to light. Let what lies beneath it be
used to teach others about the sustainability of the
earth's resources and what it means to our future.
Show them we have the technology to become great
stewards of the land.*

*Because of your education you are in the best
position to carry out this undertaking, by responsible
means, in whatever way you see fit. I know you will
make the right decisions. Because it will be yours
outright, you might also choose to build a home
there. Your future, like the view from El Mirador, will
be magnifico.*

Zara stared at the screen, fighting waves of both joy and
sorrow at seeing these precious last images of her father and
hearing his voice, traces of his Welsh lilt still audible. He used
the same words she'd uttered a week ago. *'Magnifico.'* He'd
answered her question...the why.

Her father had been as much a conservationist as a builder
and did not want the beautiful beaches of the Costa del Sol
mutilated by uncontrolled mining efforts. He trusted her to do
the right thing. She was never more proud to be a Flynn. She
knew now what she would build there.

She took the drawing from the portfolio case, went out into
the hall and across the reception area. Pilar and two of the
office girls immediately stopped talking as she passed by, all

three with the same sheepish grin on their faces. Curious, but too overwhelmed by emotion to ask questions, she continued on to Dave's office. The door stood open but she knocked anyway.

"Excuse me, Mr. Parker?"

At his desk, Dave finished a phone call. He hung up and looked at her, bemused. "Why yes, Miss Flynn?" She closed the door behind her.

"My mother is coming on Friday."

"So I heard. Does this mean you've come to a decision?" He meant about staying in Spain.

"Yes." She stood still. Concerned, he moved out from behind his desk and leaned on the desktop, holding out his hand for her. She grasped it with her left hand and held up the drawing in her right. Her father's sketch for the villa 'La Dulce Zara.'

"This was meant for me, for us. This is what I want to build at El Mirador. A home."

Dave held the sketch along with her. The artist signature in the title block read 'Tristan B. Flynn.' Zara felt her heart begin to swell, as if it had sprouted wings and would take flight from her body at any moment. *I just said 'us.'*

She'd found her why and it included Dave. His eyes gave him away, their blue color intensifying beneath gathering tears. He brought her close and held her so tight she could barely breathe.

"You're the boss," he said, his voice breaking. Then he kissed her with all the passion that had grown between them.

When their lips parted, Zara was out of breath. "They're going to wonder what we're doing in here," she said with a soft laugh.

"No they won't," he said. "They already know."

EPILOGUE

March, 1973

Marlena held out the newborn in her arms for Tristan to see. Most people would say that a baby's resemblance to a parent wouldn't be noticeable so soon after birth. Yet he could already recognize the strong features of Ariel Torres in the tiny boy's face.

"My aunt has name him Jorge," she said, in her beginner English. "She love him very much." Tristan felt glad the child's mother had accepted him after all, and that she herself had not become an outcast.

Still a vivid memory, he'd managed to drag the pregnant Marcela from the flames that engulfed El Mirador that night and could recall the sickening smell of burning flesh even now.

At the time, he worried that saving her might be a mistake-- and bringing her back to her family in Zaragoza an even bigger mistake. But he learned that fate was a wily companion, for in doing so he had met her niece, Marlena.

He couldn't take his eyes off the brunette beauty, as she

stood there rocking the babe and humming a tune for him. Barely seventeen, she was his reason for coming back all these months later, because whatever his destiny might hold, Tristan knew she would be part of it.

He hadn't been able to save El Mirador. But he did save Ari, as he swore he would. Because he had saved Jorge.